PORTRAIT OF MY MOTHER
Who Posed Nude in Wartime

For Rabbi Joshua + Goldie,
with great thanks
for your warmth and
wonderful questions.

Enjoy!
Marjorie Sandor

ALSO BY MARJORIE SANDOR

The Night Gardener (1999)
A Night of Music: Stories (1989)

PORTRAIT

OF

MY MOTHER

WHO

POSED NUDE

IN WARTIME

STORIES

Marjorie Sandor

Marjorie Sandor

Sarabande Books

LOUISVILLE, KENTUCKY

No part of this book may be reproduced without written permission of the publisher. Please direct inquiries to:

Managing Editor
Sarabande Books, Inc.
2234 Dundee Road, Suite 200
Louisville, KY 40205

LIBRARY OF CONGRESS CATALOGING-IN-PUBLICATION DATA

Sandor, Marjorie.
    Portrait of my mother, who posed nude in wartime : stories / by Marjorie
Sandor. — 1st ed.
    p.   cm.
    ISBN 1-889330-83-3 (cloth : alk. paper) — ISBN 1-889330-82-5 (pbk. : alk. paper)
1. Domestic fiction, American.   I. Title.
PS3569.A5195P67 2003
813'.54—dc21   2002009887

Cover image: Hopper, Edward. *New York Movie.* (1939) Oil on canvas, 32 ¼ x 40 ⅛" (81.9 x 101.9 cm). The Museum of Modern Art, New York. Given anonymously. Photograph © 2002 The Museum of Modern Art, New York.

Manufactured in the United States of America.
This book is printed on acid-free paper.

Sarabande Books is a nonprofit literary organization.

NATIONAL
ENDOWMENT
FOR THE ARTS

This project is supported in part by an award from the National Endowment for the Arts, and by a grant from the Kentucky Arts Council, a state agency of the Education, Arts, and Humanities Cabinet.

FIRST EDITION

For Tracy

TABLE OF CONTENTS

———

Legend
11

Capacity
21

Elegy for Miss Beagle
43

Orphan of Love
63

Portrait of My Mother, Who Posed Nude in Wartime
87

The Handcuff King
113

Annunciation
135

God's Spies
153

Gravity
179

Malingerer
189

The Author
213

ACKNOWLEDGMENTS

———

The author gratefully acknowledges
the following publications, in which these stories,
in slightly different form, first appeared:

The Georgia Review
"Elegy for Miss Beagle,"
"Orphan of Love,"
"Portrait of My Mother,
Who Posed Nude in Wartime"
"Malingerer"

Shenandoah
"Annunciation"

The Southern Review
"Capacity"

Five Points
"God's Spies"

LEGEND

———

They named her Clara. Whose idea was it? I asked my Grandma Eva once—she ran the show from day one, as far as I could tell. I pictured her selecting the name out of one of those books, *Choosing Your Child's Name and Destiny*, considering all its historical angles and possible repercussions, then telling no one, for fear of bad luck. She'd wait till she was lying back on her pillows, a little damp and faintly offended by the indignity of labor, make sure the baby was healthy, then summon her husband into the room. At such a moment, who would argue?

Surely not my grandfather. Known in their town for his modesty, his quiet good manners, for bowing to his wife's better judgment. But apparently, just as she opened her mouth to make the pronouncement, he raised his hand and said, with rabbinical authority, "She's a Clara."

I never knew Jake Shapiro—he died when my mother was nineteen—but it seems he had one quality of which Grandma Eva was genuinely afraid: a certainty that blew into their marriage like a seasonal wind—blew in, darkened his dark eyes, parted his sad Jewish lips ever so slightly, knocked the shutters of their life around a little.

He was not, otherwise, a mysterious husband.

Eva was good and tired after my mother's appearance: this baby was her fifth—and last, thank God. It had been a tough labor, and her guard was down; otherwise, there was no accounting for her lapse. "Clara," she said. "That's not bad. Nice and old-fashioned. What does it mean?"

"Light," said Jake. "Or clear. Something like that."

"You better be sure," she said. "Fifteen years from now, come to find out it means Fated One or Snake Charmer or God knows what."

She lay back again. My mother had been reluctant and slightly wicked; wanted to come out feet first or sideways—whatever would make it more difficult. Is this really my mother? What I know of her childhood would suggest the opposite: in early pictures she is such a dutiful-looking child. She is always dressed in a clean white pinafore, always has a fresh white bow riding high on her head. Look at the solemn mouth: has someone—her mother, or an aunt—told her not to smile, lest the camera steal her soul? But there's something else, too: an absent quality in the eyes, as if, any minute, her attention might wander dangerously. Of course I'm guessing, there's no evidence that my mother ever really misbehaved. But what if there was an unknown trait hiding in her from birth, like the gift the left-out fairy gave the princess, something to come true later, when there was a minute nobody was watching.

Eva must have sighed, because suddenly Jake leaned over the baby and kissed her forehead in a deliberate, ceremonial way. That was that. Named. When the certainty was upon him, he took everything as permission.

It wasn't until the middle of the second night, as Eva's breasts began to sting and swell up in that shocking way, as sudden and convincing as a premonition, that it came to her. What if *Clara* was not just any name, but belonged, in fact, to Jake's own mother, that legendary figure of whom so little—and frankly, nothing good—was known? Eva knew only that he'd been a very young boy when the mother left them all, and that his two big brothers had made a solemn vow never to speak her name again. They'd gone so far as to blot it out in heavy ink in the family Bible. Jake had told Eva this much: how, at their father's funeral, their mother had laid a hand on each of the older boys' heads, and said, "Keep an eye on Jake for me." Before they could ask where she was going, she turned, walked down a slight slope, and stepped into a black carriage that had been waiting there all along. A gloved hand—whose, they never knew—reached out and pulled her in.

Eva, telling this story, frowned at me. I was, at the time, fifteen, and she had come to live with us for the summer, to keep an eye on me while my father was ill. Clearly, she said, my parents were too distracted to instruct me in the crucial matters of life. Did I realize, for instance, that I was only a year younger than my nameless great-grandmother the year she married and became pregnant with her first? Of course her family had arranged it all: he was a professor of history in Riga; she would have a comfortable life. But still, it was none of her doing.

Eva paused, and I understood that this was supposed to be a cautionary tale, but her eyes were wide, her voice hushed and missing its usual sharpness, and so in the end I got the wrong picture. I saw not Jake's cruel mother but a vulnerable girl, a girl who had by some mishap and no will of her own borne three sons before her twentieth birthday—and who now, only now, escaped them all in a cloud of black lace. I was ashamed, but not sorry, when the coachman cracked the whip, the horses whinnied, and the carriage jerked to a start, tilting a little to one side as it rolled out of view. It was breathtaking, how a person could vanish.

Vanished was too pretty a word, said Eva. It was abandonment, pure and simple, and she hoped I was paying attention. Was I? Before I could answer, she sighed. On the other hand, she said, was it strictly necessary to wipe a person's name from history? What was it with men and their solemn vows? Of course they weren't men, they were teenaged boys, hotheaded and alone now, growing up all at once. And nobody foresaw what lay ahead: the blotting out of more names than could be dreamed. To save even one, Eva said. Even one....

I put my hand on hers, to hide my greed for the rest of the story, and waited. "So," I said.

At last she went on. It was her private opinion that the two brothers had underestimated little Jake, five years old: his potential for love, for the harboring of grief. He was always quiet, my grandfather, and probably he was that way as a child, too:

half the time you wouldn't believe he was paying attention, he was that dreamy. But probably it was the very opposite. He was taking everything in, storing it up for the journey across the Atlantic. Saving things everyone else had forgotten.

So, naturally, thinking like this in the childbed, Eva got herself into a state of worry. She didn't tell me this, but I imagine that for her, the truth, any little truth, was a dark fluttering, a pair of wings that lived and breathed beside her heart, and was now in her hands as she held little Clara. It was nothing she could describe to anybody on earth: no spectacular dreams came to visit her, with a fanfare of angelic trumpets, nor did the voices of the dead whisper in her ear—these were men's ways. So dramatic and obvious and tiresome, why did they have to proclaim everything? She frowned at me again. "You don't have crazy dreams, do you?"

"Of course not, Grandma," I said.

"That's my good girl," she replied. "That's one trait you can live without."

But wasn't she dreaming, too, feeling that ghost-girl at her bedside as she made ready to nurse: a rustling of black silk, dark moth-wings in the heart? Jake had been *her* baby: wouldn't he, naturally, be the one she'd choose to haunt? A heart broken before the age of bitterness will stay tender, open for all time.

There was something else, Eva said. Maybe it would do me good to hear it. It was something she'd never even told my mother, though there was no real reason, only that I was asking so many questions, and anyway, with my own father not in perfect health, maybe a little story was in order, by way of dis-

15

traction. So, she said, one day, long before she had any children at all, she was dusting the parlor bookcase, and noticed that the pages of an old Grammar were strangely warped, as if they'd gotten wet. She pulled it out, and discovered, inside, a tiny oval portrait of a bride and groom on the wedding day. In a heartbeat, she saw her own Jake as a small boy, all dark curls and serious-ness, sneaking this artifact out of the family album when his brothers weren't looking, surely a sin, a dangerous act. All the way across the ocean it came, secretly, alongside the famous proclama-tion of silence, and nobody had ever known.

She looked at it for a long time. At its center stood the bride, all of sixteen, in a high-necked gown, her fingers curved over the back of her husband's chair. Her eyes, beautifully long and narrow, bore a look of such somber surprise it took Eva's breath away. When she saw that face, she thought she understood why she'd left them all. She looked like nobody's mother at all, but a girl in white, still waiting for her life to begin. She'd never told Jake; she'd slipped the photograph back into the Grammar. Did he know he still had it? He always said to her, smiling: I'm simpler than you think; not a man of secrets.

Not a man of secrets. But what if we all have secrets—the forgotten kind, the kind that rise only in dreams, so hazy they can't be translated in daylight. Because my grandfather Jake, it is true, had dreams, they shook him up the way a vision would, you'd think the Messiah had come to call; only in his case they were all about love. In these, a charming, exhausted girl always figured, was always taking him somewhere—on foot, by train or tramcar—gazing into his eyes with thrilling urgency, then putting her finger to his lips and slipping away, though he cried, wait for me, wait. He had told Eva all this, confessed it as if he were not a good husband, having such dreams. But who was this girl? He didn't recognize her at all.

Eva pretended not to know, and on those mornings when he awoke with tears in his eyes, and the crushing pressure of lost love on his chest, she bowed her head and took him in her arms as if he were her child. She even let him shake a little: by tacit agreement, neither of them called it crying. She refrained from telling him that he would never meet this girl, not even in Paradise, and never told him, either, over the years of their marriage, how it hurt her that he couldn't let go. The heart of the practical woman is a beautiful ancient vase buried under rubble—the archeological team is busy elsewhere, and the earth keeps settling.

Eva believed him, that he didn't think he knew his mother's name. It would be more like him for the name itself to descend from nowhere, to present itself, gleaming and true, a fait accompli. She shivered. If it was the past that held Jake captive, it was the future that worried her; the future, that perverse and squirming bundle whose gaze tells you nothing you can count on, but watches your every move with unblinking eyes and what already looks like a faint smile, unrepentant.

She raised the baby up in her hands, the baby whose name would be Clara. The little face was fiercely flushed, as if the child had been fighting. Eva had been anemic during pregnancy, and in the last few months had eaten plenty of beef and eggs and spinach greens, just to be on the safe side. Maybe it was nothing more than that. But the baby's eyes were narrow and long, not round and buttony as Eva's baby pictures showed her own to be. Some children, she knew, were throwbacks. They bore an uncanny resemblance to some long-lost relative nobody could trace, and brought back into the world that person's worst characteristics: an impulsive nature, an impractical streak, a capacity for secrecy. There was nothing in that face to tell for sure what her character would be.

So Eva brought the baby down, cradled her properly, and made a wish. *Please be ordinary. In spite of whatever made your father name you Clara, please God, let your life be ordinary. Let nobody, nobody, notice anything out of the usual.* A small wish, but Eva found herself reciting it like a child's prayer before bedtime, fervently picturing it true. She went so far as to close her eyes. And when she opened them, she saw her husband looking at the baby with his dark sad eyes, bright with tears.

"Jake, why are you looking at her like that?" whispered Eva.

"No reason," he said. "Only making a little wish for her."

"A wish?" cried Eva. "What wish?"

That was when my mother, the baby Clara, shook her head with a wild little motion, and latched on to the breast with a terrifying *snap*.

"Mein Gott," cried Eva, sitting up so fast that the baby lost her hold. But Clara was merciless. She sank to the breast again and gave a second yank, fiercer than the one before. She pulled hard, her mouth rosy and brash with strength, pulling down the milk, hot as fire through Eva's breast, oh, her whole body, until Eva was forced to sink back onto the pillow. Jake was watching her with amazement; he did not look away, and it was too much for Eva. "He was too much for me, your grandfather," she told me. "Those tender eyes, that heart full of secrets."

"Yours is too, Grandma," I said. I meant to console her, but she gave no sign that she'd heard, only put her hand over mine, as my father would do later that summer, to let me know, as kindly as he could, that my questions would have to wait. Then my grandmother closed her eyes, and I saw she was surrendering all over again to motherhood, that condition as big and unbeatable as the sky at night, the black dome of it jammed full of beauty, stars, and trouble.

CAPACITY

By the time she was eleven, the house was deep in old-age quiet. She had tender breasts already and, my God, what looked like hips, said the Shapiro aunts, turning her this way and that in the kitchen. Her mother and the aunts kept her well-surrounded: no dark fact could break into this picture, dirty it up or confuse it. But it was 1936, and her father's store was in trouble, and something else was wrong. His eyesight was failing, and he got up to pee five times a night. Nobody spoke of it. The aunts swarmed in her mother's parlor, clutching Clara to their bosoms, giving her big smacking kisses. "Doll," they called her, and "Cutie-pie," words that didn't suit her then, that never would. She felt, at the time, *shunned* by life, as if it didn't think her worth the effort, and was deliberately keeping away.

It made her wild, that feeling. She imagined clawing her way out of Aunt Bea's grasp, kicking over her mother's Havilland dessert set, putting her boot down on a neighbor-lady's gloved fingers. But this was a secret, cherished craziness; the opposite was what showed. One day, she overheard two girls in the class-room refer to her as "Miss Goody-Two-Shoes," and felt, for the first time, the icy slow pull of a certain kind of anger. She stepped neatly past the girls and sat down at her desk, but she couldn't forget. The scene rose up when it saw fit: in the bleak hollows of a hot afternoon, or deep in the ticking night, making the curves of her new window shade, its dainty fringed balls, go foreign, ugly, alive.

The invitation to English Lake rescued her. It came in August from Elaine, a newly married cousin in Indianapolis, and was addressed, with breathtaking formality, only to her. The cream-colored envelope looked just like the one the wedding invitation had come in, and in loopy handwriting said: *Picnics, rowing, bring a big straw hat!* Clara, it appeared, had been singled out by the only attractive person in the family.

Elaine had short blue-black hair and almond eyes, skin so pale it looked like cold, veined marble in sunlight. The Shapiro aunts had never liked her looks. Before the wedding, Clara had heard them in the kitchen: did anyone notice the way Elaine was allowed to wear her hair, smooth as a cap to her earlobes and the bangs cut straight across? Aunt Bea said, "Somewhere between Cleopatra and a helpless child—she's asking for it," and when Clara said, "What's she asking for?" her mother shook her head. "Enough, Bea," she'd said. And that was that.

Clara's own experience of Elaine had been confined to big

occasions: a glimpse across a sea of lawn or synagogue chairs; a pale dress and slim pumps, that brief black stamp of hair so unlike anyone's in their pale-haired family. Then, at the wedding itself, Elaine had briefly taken notice of her. As she was carried past in her bridal chair, she'd leaned down and whispered, "Don't listen to anybody." Clara flushed with pleasure—the mystery of this remark was supreme—and bowed her head as Elaine floated away, still laughing.

And now English Lake. It was only fifty miles away, but a place she'd never been. From the name, she imagined croquet hoops on a great green lawn, and her cousin Elaine reclining on a chaise longue, her delicate features hidden by a hat, teaching her how to be subtle with boys. She'd be in a chaise longue, too, right next to Elaine, glancing up from her book to see a young man watching her intently.

She waited for her mother to say the inevitable, "By yourself? She's not thinking straight—doesn't she know you're still a child?" But her mother held the invitation in her hand a long minute, and then sighed. "I think so, this time," she said. "A good arrangement all around." Her face was soft, almost pleading. "Would you like to go?"

Clara contained herself, nodded quietly. This was not like her mother, who watched her smallest movements, who worried about her friends, and then about her lack of friends, until it seemed easier to hide in her room with a book and forget the whole business. And it was not like her mother, either, to let Clara choose her own outfit for the train ride, the clothes to be packed in her overnight bag. Like a dream, all of it. The night before the appointed day, still picturing the great lawn and the croquet hoops, she spread her white cherry-sprigged dress on the bed with a creamy sweater. It looked funny there, as if somebody were in it already, laid out for death. Ugh, crazy, she felt the ugly sensation again, a twisted root that kept shooting up surprises. She got into her nightie, and in her secret Girl's Diary wrote, quite simply, "I'm probably crazy. With any luck, I'll be dead by thirty." Then, in her best school cursive, the name *English Lake* three times. She felt much better and fell right asleep.

HOT, MURDEROUSLY HOT. The dress clings to her in the silence that has followed her from her own house to the sidewalk on Sycamore Street, to Main, to the train station. She can feel people watching her through their lace curtains, watching her legs, her breasts too big for her age. At least nobody leans out a window to shout, "Where ya off to, Doll, with your little satchel?" For once she slips smoothly through, and at the station window buys a ticket without being lured into conversation. Though surely there are other passengers, she will always remember the train as fantastically empty, the pure thing to remember about this trip, how for an hour she forgot about being watched, and looked out at the world with its untouched future, the known houses and buildings flung backward, and her real life opening somewhere just ahead, slow and magical and private. She felt clean, unjangled: there were pears to buy, each one wrapped in tissue-paper, and red-striped sacks of peanuts, and the conductor swayed through the car touching the back of each seat like a blessing, singing the names of towns. The houses along the tracks surprised her a little; sad little shacks, or what looked like old garages open to the air, and underwear on clotheslines, right out in the open. A man in overalls held a beer bottle high in salute as they passed. She waved back, and as if this were the signal he'd been waiting for, he opened his mouth to show he had no teeth. She closed her eyes, but even then he wouldn't go away.

There was no real station, no real town, just a stone house, and the conductor singing a name she didn't know. But he stopped and touched her shoulder and said, "That would be you, Miss." She searched through the windows for a slim, bridal beauty, but there was only a man in a white shirt and dark trousers, scanning the windows of the train. His mouth was set in a brief line of cold displeasure, and she knew, absolutely, that it had something to do with her. As she stepped down off the train in her cherry-sprigged dress, she lost her footing, and barely caught the handrail in time. There was only the glaring white background of the dress, the bloom of too-pink cherries with their fragile stems, her own pale legs and white anklets and saddle shoes—why hadn't her mother stopped her from wearing this?

"Careful now," said the conductor.

"I'm waiting for my cousin," she began.

"You're waiting for me," said the man on the platform, sighing. "I'm the husband."

Something in her began to crumble. She hadn't paid attention to the bridegroom at Elaine's wedding. He was simply one more man in a dark suit, either at Elaine's side or in a cluster of other men. She *had* paid attention to the kiss, not to him exactly, but to the way he swooped roughly in and covered Elaine's face so you couldn't see. It gave her a flutter, a warmth under her skin, the way she got sometimes at movies. The Shapiro aunts had tittered later. "He's a bit coarse," one said, and another added, "After the honeymoon, she'll know better. We'll all know better." When she'd asked her mother if he was a nice person, her mother bit her lip and turned away. "Handsome is as handsome does."

Was this man supposed to be handsome? Because now, in the ordinary light of afternoon, his cheeks appeared pink and faintly puffy, babyish and old at once. She was wracked by a burst of heat, pouring through her veins; could this be seen, somehow, on her skin? But he had taken her satchel out of her hand and was already walking away, off to a weedy lot, where a shining brown automobile with no top waited.

"Thank you," she said, and instantly regretted it, the sound of her own voice weak as a child's. The car comforted her briefly: she'd seen it decorated with tin cans and crepe paper at the wedding, open to the air. "Very snazzy," her mother had said, frowning about that, too.

On the drive, he offered no small talk, but dropped her down into a silence that felt intimate and attractively stubborn. It occurred to her that he had been sent on exactly the sort of errand he most despised. She wanted to comfort him as she'd seen her mother do with her father, lay her hand on his arm and say, "I'm sorry you have to play chauffeur." No, she thought, and then remembered another phrase of her mother's: "When in doubt, keep your mouth shut."

Field after yellow field, the buzz of cicadas. At last they turned onto a dirt road and began to drive under big oaks and sycamores, a pretty, filtered light. Still, it was hard to believe in a lake. After a time, she realized she was hot, and wet under the arms, and he absolutely wouldn't speak. Then the husband—she couldn't remember his first name—swerved the car suddenly off to a side road, and said tersely, "Here you are."

There were more trees here, at least, clusters of big oaks, and a curved row of wooden cottages. She was briefly restored by the sight of the cottages, with their flower beds and a little grassy lawn out front, but as they drove up, something new was wrong. A rotten smell lifted from among the trees, the sandy soil, the edge of the lake itself. The husband didn't seem to care: he opened the car door formally, but once she was out, slammed it abruptly and strode away. She stood like a fool beside the flowers, then crouched closer. "Are these geraniums?" she called out. No one answered—for a terrible moment she thought no one else was there. Where was Elaine? What if she was the victim of an elaborate hoax? Or maybe the husband was mad at Elaine, too, or maybe she was holding herself aloof from him, sulking in the cabin somewhere, and that was why he was so quiet, so sullen.

"Smells like rotten eggs, doesn't it?" A young man or boy— maybe only in high school—stood in the doorway. He didn't wait for her to answer. "It's sulfur," he said. "There's hot springs under us, all over here, so it stinks like Hell. I think that's how they could afford it. Welcome to the palace, may I take your wraps?" One of his front teeth was capped, and flashed silver: there was something pleasantly idiotic, disarming about it, Clara couldn't say what, but it was a relief from the cold, silent judgment of the husband—Herb, Herb Rifkin, that was right, now she remembered. Still, she missed him being there. His silence felt strangely correct, as if she'd asked for too much in the first place. It was, in its own way, nourishing and real, like a finger pressed against a bruise she hadn't known was there before.

"Come on in," the boy said. "Her highness is seriously bored."

Elaine was in fact lying stretched out on a sofa, and barely raised her head as Clara walked up. Clara felt again that crumbling sensation, for the unforgiving light was working on Elaine's skin, too, turning it waxy pale, and her eyes, so dark they absorbed all light, were shadowed beneath. And the cottage! It had been cheaply, haphazardly decorated with cast-off lamps and sofas, everything mustard-colored or a muddy green, and had a devastated, false feel, like a concocted setup, a façade. She looked all around. There was no accounting for the absurd distance between the formal invitation and this plaid sofa, these two men, the graceful languor of the bride gone flat.

Her feeling that the whole thing was a trick, a joke, came back like a wave of light. She saw her mother holding the invitation, considering, *a good arrangement all around*. What if her own mother was in on it, but not in the way she'd hoped, but rather to teach her some sort of lesson about being a woman—that would make more sense, but why? She had done nothing to show that she needed a lesson. She saw another door, and there was such a strained silence in the room that for a moment she let herself believe that twenty people were behind it, dressed in party clothes, waiting to greet her with a great shout of "Surprise!" Then it would all make sense, and whatever was building up would dissolve like a dream.

But the door remained a door. If anyone was behind it, it was Herb Rifkin, surly and fully himself, smoking, or playing a hand of solitaire, thinking nothing of them. His absence pulsed in her blood. It meant something, and none of this did; she could not say why. The other guest introduced himself. Ed Smith, he said, little brother of a buddy of Herb's. "You could say I'm your personal Boy Scout," he said, with a brief laugh. It made her nervous. She had no idea what it meant or how she should respond, so she nodded. This seemed to relax Ed a bit. He bent low over something on the floor—a black case—and brought out a silver trumpet. He leaned slightly backward and let his fingers, long and pale, rush over the valves. What a relief it was to watch him, his eyes closed, his attention given wholly to this thing. When he was done, he grinned at her, and the silver tooth glinted at her again, so directly she flushed and had to look away.

And suddenly there was Herb. She'd missed the moment of his return. He leaned against the bedroom door and she felt it again, the dark pull of his unhappiness, coming her way.

"How do you plan to entertain your cousin, now that she's here?" he said.

"I don't need entertaining," Clara said, but Elaine was rousing herself, propping herself up on one elbow.

"I think there's a rowboat," she said, yawning. "Or lunch—does that sound good?"

"We can't all fit," said Herb. "And it's too early for lunch."

Elaine looked at him plaintively, but he put up a hand like a traffic cop.

"Let the kids go. You don't have to be in on every little thing."

"Herb—"

"Baby," he said. "We can't all fit in the boat. We'd have to take turns." Did he mean to be insulting? What came off of him was not exactly meanness, but more like cruel, bracing intelligence. There was no flicker of hurt or surprise in Elaine's eyes; she met his gaze exactly. Clara realized she'd have been sobbing already, sobbing and clawing at his T-shirt, or simply lurching out the door to freedom. *Baby*, he'd called her.

The silence in the room was different from the muffled, invalid quiet of her house. Here there was a jagged buzz, like circus music played in the wrong key. No one else seemed dismayed.

"Well," she said. "I'm ready to do *something*." She must have bowed her head submissively, for Herb laughed. "That's a good girl. Wish your damned cousin was that easy."

"I'm not easy," Clara said, but Herb wasn't paying attention. He was leaning over the couch, leaning over Elaine, hiding her from view the way he had during the wedding kiss, and down in her belly Clara felt a dark flare of heat, like a match struck, slowly dying out. Ed Smith lifted the trumpet to his lips and blew a long, sad reveille on his trumpet, but Herb and Elaine ignored the joke, as if he were, in fact, simply a musician they'd hired for the scene. *She* wasn't there at all—their kiss blotted her out completely. Now Elaine was rousing herself, putting her arms around Herb's neck, letting him lift her in his arms as if she were a child. Herb headed for the bedroom door and kicked it open with his foot.

"We'll eat when you come back," said Elaine, laughing weakly, as Herb used his hip to push open the door, into the room Clara was afraid to look at, now that she might have. Ed was standing at the cabin door, holding it open with a look of grim gallantry.

"Let's go, kid, pronto," he said, and she realized she'd been utterly blank, gone. He had somehow put his trumpet away, and she'd missed that, too.

"M'lady," he said sternly, still holding open the door.

THE LAKE WAS LIKE ANY LAKE in flat country on a hot August day: not really blue, but a milky gray, the birdsong muffled, the same silence as in the cabin. It wanted her now, that silence. It drank from her throat and arms, the tender backs of her knees. The water lapped against the dock but was otherwise dead still as she stepped carefully into the boat, Ed Smith holding it steady. As they shoved off, the water seemed to knock at the hull like somebody at the door, polite but secretly insisting. The sky, just like the water, was that milky, undefined color, like an old land-scape painting, the kind that's called *Storm Approaching*. In this painting, the sky is white, with only the faintest outlines of thunderheads billowing up somewhere far away. You have to look a long time to see them, as if the painter has made them faint on purpose, refusing the drama. The thing is, once you see them, their gray curved outlines, you can see almost nothing else. She'd seen one in a schoolbook; it said the painter had actually used his thumb to spread the watercolors. Thinking about the artist's thumb, the milky spread of color, sent another wave of sickening light through her.

It wasn't unfamiliar, this color, this feeling. It belonged to hot summer days in her own life, days when she'd come into the house from playing, not saddened, for once, by the quiet and the dark. And for a moment she'd be happy: the wood floor was cool on her bare feet and there was this brief illusion that the low prison of sky had vanished, and she was free. Then a little sound would break in—a toilet flushing, a tap turned on, a door handle turned—and she would see her father in the hall, home early from the store again, shuffling around the corner, the tail of his nightshirt disappearing last. She stood still, listening hard, but there was nothing more. He had gone back to bed. Later her mother would come out into the parlor and put a hand on her arm. "Can you go outside and play a little more?" she'd say. "Papa needs to rest." And she'd leave the house again, with no plan, nowhere to go but outside into the hot light that had no end.

This was what she felt now, alone with the silver-toothed boy on the lake. He rowed steadily, as strangely colorless as the lake and the day. He was too pale for summer. If somebody painted him, he'd be blue-white, with a scrap of pale blue wetted-down hair and pale eyes.

Rowing, thank God. As long as he was silent, busy with the work of rowing, she felt all right, though faintly aware that she was trying to survive something, the length of time it would take them to get back to shore. She found herself hoping he'd just row, and never say a word to her the whole time. Not one word.

But no sooner had she thought this, of course, than he opened his mouth. The tooth glinted dully, like old pewter, no longer pleasant or silly. She was alone in a boat with a *boy*—and out of nowhere she recalled a phrase of her mother's, "They have a capacity"—though for what, her mother had not said. She remembered only the way her mother had snapped her fingers and said, "Like a match!" *Capacity.* The word itself was a gap, a rip in the blank surface of the lake.

She must have done something—shifted in her seat, or looked away suddenly—something, anyway, that communicated her fear to him. She might have moved her feet without thinking, but in any case he was leaning back with the oars, and she saw his pale arms twitch with the pull; just at his ribs the T-shirt lifted slightly and fell, lifted and fell, until a moment when she snapped out of it. She'd been staring again. And now he looked back at her, that colorless passive gaze, and in what seemed a mere second, let go the oars and stripped off his shirt.

"Apologies," he said, grinning. "If apologies are in order."

Her heart thrummed with a high, hot speed. "Pardon," she said, to gain time. It was like a dream, the kind where you're on stage, in a play of some sort, and everybody knows their lines but you. She looked out at the lake, but it defied her, too. It had transformed into a rippled silver sheet, like the corrugated metal of those houses by the train tracks.

"Elaine wasn't kidding about you," he said. "And it's okay, you don't have to play Miss Priss with me."

Now she looked out at the lake in earnest, trying to imagine what Elaine had said about her. She barely knew Elaine, what could she possibly say that would be true? In accordance with the strange plot, the shoreline had vanished. Of course he might simply be rowing them farther out, to a place where they could never be seen, never be heard. The disappearance of the shore, its weeds and ferns and scrubby trees, seemed more terrible than anything.

He stood up and tugged lightly at his pants, and knowledge flooded her veins. Later it would dawn on her that he might have been merely readjusting himself on the seat. But not then. Surely he was about to push her into the wet puddle at the bottom of the boat, covering her with his body out where nobody could see. There would be his man's thing, briefly exposed, then a terrible pressure, sharp as a knife. She knew this absolutely.

Her speed amazed her. It was as if some force had come to her aid, for a light breeze from nowhere sprang up, rocking them, giving her the idea. She planted her feet slightly apart, with a kind of delicate brilliant pleasure, a hot light in her ribs, and ever so gently began to rock the boat side to side, side to side, the way, she thought, a cradle should be rocked. Only the more she rocked, the more she felt the pleasure of doing it, its rhythmic, musical purity. This, and only this, was right.

"Hey, *hey*," said Ed Smith, gripping the sides of the boat, but she rocked one great snap harder, and over he went, right over the side, crashing heavily into the water.

He thrashed and lifted his head like a dog's, then spat hugely at the side of the boat, but she couldn't be stopped now. The feeling was new, and big, a blue flame fanning itself higher and higher, pure and exact. She saw her mother again, holding the invitation. She saw Herb at the station, and Elaine lying like an opera star on the couch. *No,* she thought wildly. What an amazing word, it was, standing all alone, a sword, a flame, gorgeous and all hers.

"Hey, come on, hey," he cried. "Damn it, I forgot your name. You're nuts, bring the boat over here."

"No," she said. "You can swim."

She got herself into the rower's seat, grasped the oars, and began to make for shore, though she had no idea, in that milky light, where shore might be.

SHE FOUND IT SOONER than she thought she would, and felt, immediately, the first twinge of exhaustion and disappointment, a faint taste of metal in the mouth. No matter what she did next, it wouldn't be the end of the story. She was pretty sure she hadn't killed him, but she didn't trust the weird silence of the lake, either. Possibly he had some supernatural ability to hold his breath, and would, at any minute, appear beneath the boat and topple her. This was why she got out when she did, abandoned the boat and wound up in the muddy, tangled grasses along the shore, soaked to the waist, covered with tiny bits of green muck, as if every sticky thing in the lake had attached itself to her. She looked down at her dress, the soaked bodice gone pink from cherries, and began to shake. Anybody who saw her now would know that she was a helpless, muddy girl who'd nearly been violated, and was now lost in an unfamiliar place without anyone she really knew. Wouldn't they? Tears—genuine enough—came up hot behind her eyes.

She emerged onto dry land, a disappointing little glade of scrub oaks. What was she expecting? A medieval forest, great towering trees and shafts of sunlight, a deep contrast of light and dark? Because it was starting to feel exactly the opposite: grimy and confusing and meaningless. Her own act kept rising up instead of Ed Smith's. It dawned on her now that he, in fact, had committed no act—nothing at all.

Then, cabin rooftops, not far away at all, but cut off from her by brambles and high grass. She stopped walking then, and stood still a moment, trying to get her legs to stop trembling, and that was when she heard it, felt it under her feet: a deep, regular thudding behind her, from the direction of the lake. It had to be. She felt a wretched calm, flatly neutral, as if her life were already over. It was almost a relief. Dead by thirty. She'd known it, of course. And this was what her mother meant—*capacity*—and she thought, this is what must come, this, and nothing else. She turned to face it—nothing less than her deserved destiny of violent ravagement and death by God knows what enormous monster—and saw a cow. It was a dirty white cow, chewing and moving steadily forward, glancing at her sideways with a doleful, irritated look. The relief was tremendous, as if a trigger had been touched, and she screamed, to her own ears a goofy horror-show scream that came back at her from the lake, for the whole world to hear.

The cow looked at her long and slow. It summed her up, dismissed her, then swung its head away and began to eat. For a moment she stood stunned, her insufficiency trembling and real, and then she ran—ran straight out of the glade and onto a road.

It had been there all along, the road. And the cottages themselves were within plain view. She must have been looking at another group of them. As she came closer, she heard dishes clattering, a child's sudden cry. It was her own rowing, not Ed

Smith's, that had carried her straight back to them, the one time in her life that she needed to be missed, lost for several hours in the wilderness.

But Ed Smith was already at the cottage when she got there, and Elaine was lying on the couch again, with Herb leaning over her. For a split second she wondered if she'd dreamed it all—everything from the moment of Herb's lifting Elaine from the couch and carrying her off—because Elaine looked as pale and miserably self-absorbed as before. If there was anything different, it was that they were all looking at *her* now, with barely contained smiles. It didn't take long for her to realize that the story—Ed's version of it, anyway—had long since been told, and they had feasted on it, had a good laugh, and were already bored, finished, ready to play cards and eat a big lunch. She thought dimly of maidens, virgins, the way they were sacrificed in the old days, as part of a special festival of harvest. You burned her with special ceremony, and then ate a big dinner.

"Thank you for a nice time," she said. "I'm leaving now."

Ed was grinning openly at her now, and she saw that he wasn't even angry, that the biggest action of her life was a joke to him, its outcome known all along. It seemed crucial to her dignity, to whatever hope she had of being believed back home, not to look at him ever again. It seemed important not to look at anyone, though she felt, dimly, that Elaine was trying to get her attention, picking up a handkerchief and blowing her nose daintily, showily, like some crazy echo of Ed's reveille. It was distracting, as was the faint recognition that Elaine's robe was slightly open, showing her pale thigh, and on it, a small dark-blue stain, like a birthmark, or ink. It made her feel a little sick; why didn't Elaine cover it up?

"I really must go," she said. "Thank you for inviting me," she added, holding herself erect.

"Thank my wife," said Herb, shrugging. "You want to clean up before you go?"

She was practically dizzy. Elaine hadn't paid any attention to her at all. She was practically invisible in Elaine's eyes.

"Why did you invite me?" she cried.

Elaine raised herself on one elbow, and for a split second, looked as if she might speak. Then, to Clara's amazement, she fell back on the couch, and a single tear came down her cheek.

Herb looked at Elaine, and it seemed to Clara that his cheeks reddened. "Listen, kid, never mind. I'll give you a lift."

"I'm not a kid. And I can get there on my own."

He sighed. "What is it with this family? I'll get the keys." She nodded without looking at him, and collected her things. In her satchel was a change of clothes, but she didn't want to change anything—why? To punish Elaine, and to give her mother the full show of her bravery? She only knew that she wanted to stay in the muddy dress as long as possible.

On the way to the station, he never looked at her. She knew this, though she kept her own head rigidly still, facing out the window the whole time. At the station he opened the door for her, and asked, in a curt voice, if she had a ticket. "Of course," she said. Then, for a moment, he said nothing, and silence hung like a third party between them. She was aware of nothing but his body, his shoulders and arms, even the slight softness of his belly under his shirt. His mouth. The swiftness and surprise of the way he'd lifted Elaine from the couch. She shivered, and looked away, afraid he'd see.

"I need to ask you something," he said, his voice suddenly warm, and directed only at her. She nodded. "Okay," he said. "Don't tell your mother about Elaine, the crying and so on. It'll just complicate things for us."

She nodded again. It was hard, with him so close, to think about Elaine. She kept fading from the picture. All she wanted was for him to say one thing about what had happened to *her*. She tried to will him to. But he only laid his hand on her shoulder, a brief heat through her sleeve. He tipped his hat and turned to go.

She kept her head high all the way to the platform, and sat down to wait without looking back. And though he was long gone by then, she was careful, as she boarded the train, to lift her feet. Not until the train was safely out of the station, and the conductor was standing beside her, asking for her ticket, did she begin to tremble. It was the same conductor as before! As she handed him her ticket, he tilted his head at her so familiarly that she broke into sobs. "I fell in the lake," she said. "I was pushed—"

"That's all right, young Miss," he said, with a little smile. "You're miles from the water now."

Then he was gone, and the trip reversed itself, the repetition of houses and shacks and garages, no one outside now, and she was glad. She kept trying to call up the purity of the first ride, before anything, but with no warning, it was Elaine who was with her, nothing would come but a picture of Elaine lying down, crying in front of her, as if she'd been trying to send a message without speaking. She saw herself, too, in her muddy virgin's costume, the way she'd stood in the middle of the room trying to look angry and offended. Her own story fell away, leaving only Elaine, and the message she'd failed to grasp. Her own nod of complicity, the heat of Herb's palm through her sleeve.

Only now. In the dark, on the train, she sees what she's capable of, and even as she sees it, she can already feel herself being carried away from it, back into safety, blindness. So for once she's glad no one knows she's coming, that no one is there to see her shame. She can feel its contours, its life inside of her. She'd like to feel it, all alone, a little longer. She sees herself as a camera would: a girl disembarking from a train in a muddy dress with threads of algae hanging down, her white narrow face with its dark eyes, its full lips. Its terrible capacity. Angel, specter, ghost of her own life, she moves down Sycamore Street, glad to be outside all those lives and windows. A woman walks from one room into the next. It is a house she knows, but she can't think of the name of the woman leaning over the chair, folding a blanket. The name will not come to her, the name doesn't seem to matter, only the way the light strikes at the pale underside of the woman's arm.

In this state she walks right past her own house. It takes her ages to realize it, and to walk back, trying to hold onto the truth as it slips down through her body, and away. There are no lights on in her house—it is the only one on her street already dark— and the wide feeling inside her is beginning to fail. But she holds onto it as she goes around to the back door, stepping over the threshold into the life her parents inhabit without her. A creak on the stairs: they have heard her. Soon enough she'll surrender to habit, telling her story, with all its false childish drama, and forgetting all about Elaine, though the sense that she has missed something crucial, something true, will be with her for life.

Her mother is in the hall now, feeling the wall for the light-switch. It's still dark, but Clara sees the sad curve of her shoulders, the way the fingers tremble against the wall. "Clara, child, is it you?" cries her mother, and Clara hears the familiar high edge of her panic. But something else now, too. The coming grief, the burden of secrets.

Sudden light, and her mother's voice again, like a tide coming. "My God, sweetheart, what happened? We weren't expecting you."

"I know, Mother," says Clara, beginning to cry. "But here I am."

ELEGY FOR
MISS BEAGLE

I t was a year of maiden-lady suicides. A schoolteacher here, a piano mistress there, and always a name you'd hate to have: Miss Winifred Muckler, Miss Ione Hicks, and then, Miss Ella Beagle—my mother's teacher for Advanced Piano. It was 1938, a college town in Indiana. Picture the starched blouse, the wilted satin bow at the neck, and then, what nobody ever expects: eyes full of a clear crazy light—like the eyes of outlaws in old picture books—making you wonder what they've seen.

"Don't start with the romance," says my mother. "It's the photographer's flash—all the old pictures look like that." Miss Beagle, she reminds me, was impoverished, lived alone in a small apartment on the second floor of a partitioned house; she had no family, no people that anybody knew. In those days you could safely choose a piano teacher by name alone, and from such a name as this, Grandmother Eva got what she could: that this teacher was local, plain, had never had a love affair or a year at the Sorbonne—nothing to give a young girl ideas. And Jewish, just like us, though with the name of a little dog surely something had gone wrong at Ellis Island. In such matters my grandmother was legendary. "It's nothing, just an instinct," she used to say to us. "Down it comes, straight through the generations without a hitch, until we get to your mother."

My mother, their little girl. There's not much to go on; a mother will only tell you certain things. She says now that I have a daughter of my own I'll be the same. But what if they spoiled her a little, without realizing, then had to clamp down? What if, at twelve, she was sneaking trashy books into the house; at thirteen, sneaking out with silk stockings under the black tights. Grandfather Jacob was already sick by then with diabetes, and Eva would have kept the house dark and quiet straight through summer, as if the sunlight and the gaudy elms would speed him into his grave. Who knows why, but my grandmother worried most during brilliant weather—"Trust me," she'd say, "it's just part of the instinct."

But my mother: here she is at thirteen, still blind to the dull daily facts of adult misery. Never mind that her house smells of rubbing alcohol—no, she detects something sinister and interesting underneath, something sweet and foul. Her childish imagination connects it to the Yiddish newspapers piling up on the sideboard, the dining-room table—all those spiky letters crammed together on the page, not like any normal language. At thirteen, she's still fantasizing about being orphaned, or discovering an extra child locked up in the attic, or, at the very least, finding out that her daddy has a nasty sex-disease brought from Europe years ago. What she's really hoping for, she can't yet know, but what would it feel like to stand on the verge of knowledge in a house like that: tantalized by the dark, kept innocent of the history that, in her parents' own childhoods, had reached out like a pair of dirty hands. But my mother's just a kid, a sheltered American girl, stranded in a dark house. So when nobody's looking, she sneaks a glance at *The Family Medical Guide* and traces the tiny print under Sexually Communicated Diseases: dizziness, delirium, gradual loss of sight. Pustules, papules, squamous lesions—these she hasn't noticed yet, maybe later.

YOU CAN IMAGINE HOW, for a mother, all this would lead to piano lessons, and how, for a daughter, the mild spring air outside such a house would seem a dazzling gift, a herald of some wild open world. The sun hurts your eyes when you step out, but you're glad—you could run and run. Only she can't. It's the first day of the new lessons, and Eva's hand is on her arm, Eva is giving her a first-day basket of fruit and flowers to carry to the new teacher— a big, lavish basket, the kind the ladies of the synagogue charity league give to new Jewish families in town. So my mother steps onto the sidewalk wearing a dress of dotted swiss, white gloves, ankle socks, and saddle shoes—all of which Eva had laid out on the bed an hour ahead of time, as if for a wedding or a funeral. "It pays to make a nice impression," she said, giving my mother her famous bleak look, the steady gaze that always stunned a child into obedience.

Down the street they go, Eva's hand firmly gripping my mother's wrist. At the rickety outside stairs Eva points up and my mother ascends—a child in a fairy tale, mortified by the basket of fruit. Halfway up a plank jiggles under her foot like a baby tooth come loose, and she is so nervous and sheltered that even this makes her spine and fingertips burn, as well as the low hollow place for which she has no name, since Eva calls it "down there" if she refers to it at all. On the loose stair my mother daydreams a split-second of escape, herself a wild girl running down the shady street in a sheer nightgown, meeting a handsome boy, getting on a train—these things somehow go together. But it's no use—she's at the top, gripping the basket. Eva, down below, shoves at the air with a gloved hand. That's all it takes: jolted out of her fantasy, my mother knocks on the door.

A NARROW KITCHEN, A TRAGIC LIFE—that's what she tells me now, how a kitchen can tell the whole story. It's in the stale smell of boiled egg and tinned vegetables, the single saucepan poised in the dish rack, the stained two-burner with a tiny oven beneath. She sighs as she says this and gives me a serious look, as if it's her duty to tell me what my choices are. But at thirteen, she's onto something else. She sees, first of all, Miss Beagle's uncanny resemblance to herself: hazel eyes, freckled pale skin, a long straight nose, and, dimly, something more—a certain openness, fear and relief clearly exposed in the face from moment to moment.

At the front door Miss Beagle takes her hand, and my mother looks down at it—so ridiculously small and pale cradled in Miss Beagle's, whose fingers are as muscular as a carpenter's, the veins raised like mountain ranges on a map. Miss Beagle looks at my mother over the fat oranges, the daffodils with their wagging heads. "The ladies of the Sisterhood are at it again," she says, and leads my mother into her tiny kitchen, offers cookies from a chipped plate. The plate trembles slightly, and the cookies are the wrong kind, too fancy, too crumbly.

"I'm no good at this," says Miss Beagle. "Why did your mother pick me, out of all of them?"

She puts a hand on my mother's arm, tries to hurry her through to the music room, but my mother won't hurry; she has spotted the piano teacher's bed, a twin bed clumsily made up with pillows to look like a couch, nothing at all like her parents' four-poster with its high mattress, its snowy chenille spread always smooth in daylight. She wants to touch the bumpy spread, a ghastly yellow, the bed narrow and strict like that of a nun or penitent. Does the teacher really get undressed and slip between its covers? Or does she maybe lie on top in a man's undershirt, smoking cigarettes late into the night, reading and thinking eccentric thoughts. My mother's heart beats wildly to think this. How can it not—in Eva's house the bedroom doors are shut at all times. To keep something in, or keep it out—this was a question you didn't ask.

But Miss Beagle is waiting. Miss Beagle is tall with a slender neck, the stately tentative step of a wading bird, and her hair is cut in a bob so severe that you can see the blue-ivory nape of her neck, angled slightly forward as if for sacrifice. Miss Beagle beckons her, holds aside a noisy curtain of colored beads, a gypsy's curtain, a fortune-teller's. My mother breathes in the difference of this place and almost immediately falls into one of her fantasies of entrapment: Miss Beagle blocking the door, sealing her in the deepest cave, a lost place where anything could happen and nobody would know. Even as she's thinking this, she hears herself say, in a voice that sounds like her mother's, "Oh! May I use your ladies' powder room?" Miss Beagle dips a little from the waist, as if taking a bow, and points it out.

So THERE'S A PRELUDE, a holding off, in Miss Beagle's lavatory. In there it's as if gifts have been laid out just for a girl: exquisite adult things and the privacy Eva would never allow. On a wicker shelf there's a black-lacquer box that opens at the press of a button to reveal eight mirrored doors, cigarettes, a Mozart minuet always in progress; a red glass dish and pestle—heavy, luxurious, all curves; and three tiny amber flasks that my mother takes down off the shelf, forgetting all about the lesson. Sitting on the toilet seat, she works the crumbling cork free to get at the scent richly foreign, not sweet at all. Bathrooms are mystery, sanctuary. They are where, in her own house, she hides from company, from her mother; where the next year she will smoke one of her father's cigars and lie down to die, heart thudding as much with the possibility of discovery as the possibility of death; where, in two years, she will lock the door and climb out the high window to kiss a college boy by the azaleas, to let him bring his chill hands up under her blouse and touch the edge of her brassiere before she lurches backward, thinking for the first time exactly as her mother wants her to: that from this little touch to the vast terror of a man unzipping his pants there is no distance at all.

But in Miss Beagle's bathroom she simply studies the first of the amber bottles with its painted Oriental scene: a man kneeling before a woman, holding her foot in his palm. It means something, she knows, but the faces of the couple are expressionless, as if to keep her from understanding.

There is a light rapping on the door.

"Just a minute," she cries.

"Take your time, Miss," says Miss Beagle with a short bark of a laugh. "It's of no moment to me."

ALL SUMMER EVA KEEPS her drapes shut tight against light and heat. Miss Beagle does the same. So my mother goes from the calculated dark of her own house into a scalding daylight and then, at Miss Beagle's, back into the dark—a richer dark. The music room is a cave within the cave: no chalk-white busts of Beethoven and Bach, no jaunty booklets of Level One, Level Two. In the middle of the room is a black baby grand, its lid closed and covered by a fringed red shawl. "A Sohmer," says Miss Beagle, her voice hushed, amazed. "As fine as any Steinway, only nobody will ever know. Even as we speak, the company is going under."

It is my mother's duty to slip off the shawl and fold it neatly over a chair. At lesson's end, she smoothes it back on again, smoothes it to perfection. The polished wood floors are unmarred, the music books arranged on two walls of shelves. A stark place, a place of pure attention, and in it Miss Beagle is transformed. Every gesture is fluid, commanding. With a sweep of her hand, she indicates the piano stool, then stands to one side in exactly the right spot so that my mother cannot directly see but seems to divine the dark panels of a skirt, the hand slightly raised to mark the tempo. "Concentrate," she says, and my mother is transformed, too. She feels herself balanced, barely, on the edge of a world only Miss Beagle knows. She is aware of everything at once: the intimate rustling of her teacher's blouse, the hand rising to bring on the crescendo, the whole world gathering into the dark story of the nocturne. "Not so much, not so much," says Miss Beagle. "The truth is never loud."

My mother wants to stay there, in that room where she has "a rare memory," and even, occasionally, "real feeling"—a room where there is nothing pressing on her but the clean force of the music, no reminders or obligations, no Eva calling her down-stairs for this or that. But the lesson is over, and Miss Beagle is holding aside the curtain of bright gypsy beads, as if to get rid of her quickly. In her free hand she holds the chipped plate, full of cookies, and oranges now, too. "Please, take something," says Miss Beagle, but my mother ignores her. As she passes through the curtain, she can't resist giving the beads an angry little tug to make them rattle.

Miss Beagle sighs, "I don't blame you." But as soon as they are out the other side, her hands tremble again, still holding the plate with its cookies, the oranges from what she calls "the basket everlasting." She laughs as she sees my mother out. "Tell your mama I'll never finish it, that I'll have to take it with me into the next world. You know, like the Egyptians."

ALL THAT AUGUST when my mother practices, there's a fast ticking in her throat and in her wrists, like Miss Beagle's metronome—

she can press a finger to her throat and feel the pulse leaping, a fierce little animal wanting out. Her father sits beside her in his morris chair, the Yiddish newspapers in his lap and his eyes closed, and Eva walks past them and says, over the music, "Don't be crazy. What can you do from America?" This is all my mother hears of Europe, of Germany in the late summer of 1938. The conversation never goes further than that when she is present, and at thirteen, who's asking for more? Everything gets translated back to the self anyway. She begins to dream clouded-up dreams, groping through room after room on her hands and knees with her eyes glued shut, and somebody says in a jokey way, *Go boldly forward into the abyss,* and she knows this is a clue to some truth she needs for her life, but at the time she has no idea *what.* All the while her eyes are stuck shut; she can't see anything but that murky, sickening red, the color of fingertips held to a light.

It's amazing, she says, how such dreams fold up, vanish without your asking—there's no way, either, of inviting them back, even if you knew to do that at thirteen. Mornings arrive and sweep away the bitter residue, as do whole days, your mother's eyes watching you, the lesson hour itself. She has taken to jumping over Miss Beagle's loose stair as if it is bad luck, and once inside Miss Beagle's apartment she asks right away to use the ladies' powder room. She can stay in there five minutes without Miss Beagle minding; she wishes she could sit there forever, just holding the little flasks to the light. The faces of the lovers—for surely they are lovers—are arrested in that moment of the foot, and remain blank, hovering on the verge of what she can't imagine.

One afternoon, when my mother loses her place for the third time, Miss Beagle presses her finger imperiously to the black-and-white page. "Sometimes I think it's barely worth the struggle," she says. "But why else does the Good Lord put talent on earth? Now listen, and get it right."

Hands swoop down on either side of my mother, the fingers spreading, webbed. It's only a chord, but a fist opens suddenly in her heart. The world folds up small as an envelope: there is only the edge of herself and the beginning of Miss Beagle. My mother keeps her head down, looking at those hands, at the dark sides of Miss Beagle's blouse like wings or a tent all around her as the chord dies out. She puts her hands tight together in her lap.

Miss Beagle sighs and walks away, pulls from the bookshelf a battered yellow volume. "I want you to move on to Brahms," she says. "Just the second movement of this, impossible enough."

EVA WOULD FEEL IT, OF COURSE—that some balance in the world has tipped. Knowledge like this flickers once and vanishes, a little gap of silence in broad daylight. It seems to be coming from everywhere at once—from the newspapers, a husband's illness, a child playing a madman's music and never getting it right. She telephones her friends, the ladies of the Sisterhood. "What is it about the world?" she asks. "You can never separate things."

Especially in the quiet hot afternoons she feels it and spends more time on the telephone. Again and again the subject of my mother's piano lessons comes up. *You should see the teacher, poor thing. Lives on canned peas, an egg once in a while for protein, no fresh fruit! No family. Beagle's a Jewish name, of course. You have a piano, and your girl is how old? It's never too late to start.* After these phone calls she feels better: one lady friend, now two, now eight, have signed their daughters up.

It is Eva who comes up with the idea of a recital, and Eva who in late September takes my mother shopping for a special dress, leads her by the wrist downtown, shoves aside the hangers, and frowns at shop assistants as if this dress is a matter of the greatest importance, a matter of survival. She follows my mother and the assistant into the dressing room and stands, arms crossed, as the woman zips and unzips gowns against my mother's back, puts a cold hand to her leg, presses a measuring tape against her hips and around her breasts. It is Eva who says with pride to the assistant: "Already she's got a nice figure. Why should we hide it?"

Black velveteen, black lace sleeves, a cinched waist. Slender pumps with a narrow toe, even a narrow heel. My mother holds perfectly still, lest Eva realize what she's done. Around and around they turn her. "I don't know," Eva says triumphantly. "Maybe it goes too far."

October, November, there is no way my mother can master the Brahms. The white page is crammed close with notes, closer every time she looks, as if they are huddling together for protection. What a crazy idea. Crazy, the way she begins to ascribe to certain chords human characteristics: B-flat major is the little man in yellow tails who won't shut up, who barks bad words at her, over and over. C minor is her father, trying to climb a ladder, and slipping down and down. And when, a week before the recital, Miss Beagle has her play it through at tempo, she hears the greater madness: at first a peaceful melody, then the melody broken and flung away. She's almost sorry when it comes back so small and peaceful at the end, and when she says this, shyly, Miss Beagle nods.

"Exactly," she says. "Maybe somebody else made him close it up all nice and neat."

"Why would they?" asks my mother.

There is a tiny silence, short as a breath—it is the first time she has asked a question, a real question, sent out beyond herself—and in answer, there comes no word, but a warm pressure, a kiss on the nape of her neck.

Something dimly flares to life—not surprise, not maidenly terror. She holds still, and in this moment before time and convention move her forward, she knows the kiss for what it is: a gratitude that can't be spoken, that can't last in the world.

But already she's coming up and out of this knowledge, back up to the place where a young girl should immediately rise from the piano stool, scoop up her books, and make her way—blinded by righteous tears—to the door. Isn't that how it's supposed to go? So why are her fingertips icy; why is *down there* a hollow bloom of light, a sudden cave where before there was none? Why is it down in her body like that? It will happen to her later in life, when she is a wife and mother, but never, never when it should. This much she has told me: never with my father, but only in the odd moment—whenever she puts her weight on a wobbling step; when she climbs a lookout for a panoramic view; on the one day in her life that she stood too close to a different man, and prayed to God to not give her any more than this, and learned that a bitter wish can always be granted.

But at Miss Beagle's she is still thirteen. She rises now, takes up her books and clutches them idiotically, theatrically to her chest. She glances at Miss Beagle's face, but Miss Beagle is holding open the door. "Go home to your mama. You're late, she'll be worried sick," she says quietly, and a sharp pain bangs once through my mother's heart, as if through a narrow, narrowing place.

There is snow the day of the recital, a light, first snow; it's a nice picture from a distance: a mother and daughter walking together in long winter coats. At Miss Beagle's the others are gathering: eight girls in velveteen and brushed corduroy, eight mothers in hats and gloves. There are lemon squares and macaroons on a tray. There is punch for the girls and coffee for their mothers, served in Eva's own wedding china (sent over the day before to spare Miss Beagle any embarrassment). The ladies themselves have brought wooden folding chairs from the synagogue, and with their hands and voices they squire Miss Beagle into one of these. *Don't trouble yourself, they say. Let us take care of everything, we're used to it!* and after a few minutes of light chatter, there are three neat rows in a semicircle, a refreshment table, and the music room looks just like the synagogue lobby after services.

There will be Bach minuets, Clementi sonatinas—lovely, easy, perfectly balanced forms. Miss Beagle has listened to these over and over, played with the same halts and errors week after week. They have turned her into a ghost who stands stiffly against the bookcase, checking her wristwatch: is it over yet, this charade? She will not sit, but thank you, thank you—her hands working against her dress, her face white and strained, maybe thinking it was smart to have hidden her cigarette box, her flasks with their Chinese lovers.

But it hardly matters, because the girls and their mothers are sharply observant, not of Miss Beagle's face with its signs of grief and lost balance but of her mauve satin dress out of some godforsaken era, a costume picked for the wrong occasion. Silver buckles gleam foolishly on her dark, heavy shoes—clip-ons she must have purchased just for the occasion. "Like a witch," whispers the girl sitting next to my mother, and the girl's mother smiles at Eva as if the goal of the recital has just been accomplished. But my mother is trembling. Suddenly she knows they will soon be laughing at her, too—they all know she is the prize pupil, a witch by association. Why can't she have a normal, beautiful teacher, the kind everybody worships? Why can't Miss Beagle step forward right now in a classy dress and delicate pumps, her feet slim and fine—step forward, hands clasped together, and say, "And now, my star pupil." My mother turns toward the girl and nods. She cannot look at Miss Beagle.

My mother plays the Brahms last. The second movement begins quietly, beautifully sad and easy. Then out of nowhere comes the fierceness, the rupture, the rebellion, and it goes on and on. Her fingers would have ached, I imagine, and her wrists, but there could be no stopping. It's a piece she'll know for the rest of her life—I've heard her humming along with a recording of it performed by some famous artist, Brendel or Horowitz. She has told me how it went that day, how she was playing surprisingly well, and then—she'd never know what—something made her glance up. She saw that Eva was frowning, lips pursed, and my mother knew suddenly that she looked ugly and crazy, that her mouth was slightly open, her eyes were roving blankly over the keys. There was a little rending, a ripping inside the music—one mistake, and another, then a galloping racket of wrongness under her hands. And then, automatically, the little early melody was back, covering over the mess. She got up and closed the piano lid.

Imagine the mothers, the daughters, all rising from their chairs. The bright false applause, the sudden swarm of voices in the little room. Eva is clapping especially hard. That my mother has failed means nothing to her; that she kept going, everything! This in itself is a good lesson. Eva comes to her side, lays a hand on her arm. "I always thought she was strange," she whispers. "What young girl could play such a thing? Go out on the stairs, get some air. Go out and come back."

IT'S DESTINY, or just the small town. As she steps out onto the landing, a boy from her school is walking past. She tosses her head so that her hair falls over one eye, like a Garbo, a Dietrich. She looks him right in the eye.

"Oh God, you heard," she says, trying out a husky voice. "What a disaster."

He smiles, gives a courtly bow. She would realize, much later, how absurd it was to think he'd heard her playing; how amazing that he went along with her act. She'd wonder, too, whatever happened to him in his life. But on the stairs at that moment she knows only that he is a romantic boy, a boy who reads too much, and that it is probably like something from a book for him, a girl in a black lacy dress calling to him from a staircase, descending, coming toward him. Overhead in the trees, two cardinals—dark red against the white snow and stark branches of Miss Beagle's yard—have set up a violent racket, and the moment holds still for her. For her! She is voluptuous and dramatic in her new dress: no daughter, no pupil, no good girl at all. She holds everything perfectly still. Then calls him over. *Hurry!* she cries.

Hurry, because the door is opening at the top of the stairs, and Miss Beagle is coming out on the landing, coming down the stairs. She is clearing her throat the way she does during a lesson at a missed note, an overstated crescendo, a failure by the student to express the ordinary human truth of the moment. Hurry, too, because three or four girls have also come out on the landing, are gathering as if for a play.

"Wait," says Miss Beagle, raising one hand against the bright snow. "Please—"

But for my mother there is no stopping. She is down in the yard with the boy now, and the world is surging and alive: the snow, red birds, the branches against the house, a dazzling silence in which Miss Beagle's shoes, tapping on the stairs, only faintly interfere. Miss Beagle has come all the way down and stands in a dirty crust of snow and grass. One shoe is sinking; Miss Beagle's stockings are getting wet.

It's the shoe, the mere thought of that shoe. My mother tosses her head again, looks at the girls above, and turns to face the boy. Her voice is harsh and low. "Kiss me," she says, "quick, like you mean it." And against the white clapboards and black winter branches of Miss Beagle's yard, he moves her backward as if they are two sleek professional dancers, and she gives him a kiss too old for either of them, a kiss from the end of a movie or a book, with which the heroine, at the height of her powers, saves a life.

THAT'S ALL IT TOOK, my mother says, and less than a week. She never had to decide whether she should go to her next lesson. The first news that Friday afternoon was that something terrible had happened in Europe. They were standing at her father's bedside, and he was reading to them from the Yiddish paper: Jewish shops looted and in flames, glass shattered in the streets.

It was getting late, almost dark. Eva announced that she had a terrible headache and was going to lie down. But then he was holding up the local paper. "Listen, in *The Courier*. It's the piano teacher." Eva didn't say a word, just took the paper out of his hands. My mother stood caught in the doorway, neither in nor out, as Eva rushed past her toward the hall telephone.

I HAVE ASKED MY MOTHER, carefully, if she knows why Miss Beagle did it, and she looks at me with the smile you give a child who thinks she's being terribly clever. "You're young," she says. "You think you've got the answer. But it's always an older story than you think." I bow my head—I'm ashamed—but on the other hand, she's angry now, and when she's angry she keeps talking past the point where she'd normally stop. "What matters," she says in this new, harsh voice, "is that Miss Beagle's death was swamped, swept under by the bulletins from Europe announcing Hitler's Kristallnacht, 'the Night of Broken Glass,' and then, when the Sisterhood ladies had a chance to think, they said she must have had family in Berlin, must have gotten a telegram that week, which was why she lit the gas. That's a kind of romance, too," she goes on. "People even use history! And their version somehow became the truth—the story you heard about Miss Beagle if you asked."

That's her way of stopping, of saying *Enough now*. She never tells an end, and I'm thinking, maybe Miss Beagle taught her that endings are false. Because it goes on and on. Eva would have felt compelled to attend to Miss Beagle's personal effects, her funeral arrangements, but she wouldn't allow my mother to go along when she and the ladies of the Sisterhood went to the apartment to do what they could. No other daughters were going, she told my mother. After all, it was such a grim business. There would be enough of that later in life. My mother tried to bargain, but Eva only said, "When you're older, you'll see."

Maybe Eva knew exactly what she was doing, just as my mother does by not finishing. Because by giving her daughter no final look, she was making sure she never stopped thinking—not about Miss Beagle but about her death, its hollow misery, its dull aftermath. There were some things you just couldn't romanticize, Grandmother Eva knew—and a lonely death was one of them. Such a thing would stick with an impressionable girl for a long time.

She was right. My mother wouldn't be able to get rid of her image of Eva and the ladies of the Sisterhood climbing the rickety steps, stepping cautiously across the loose one; of how, once inside, they would start with the kitchen, the faint smell of gas still on the air. With the efficiency of nurses they wiped down the counters and emptied the cupboard, throwing out all chipped or solitary things, right down to the basket everlasting, with its last ancient orange like a joke turned prophecy. They stripped the bed, folded up the ugly yellow spread, and unhooked the cheap beads, possibly giving each other, at this point, a knowing look. But what haunted my mother, as Eva knew it would, was not knowing what they did when they got to the lavatory and found the deep red bowl, the musical cigarette box, the three little amber flasks with their lovers. The existence of these private, inviolable things Eva would never acknowledge. She came home in the twilight, pale and haggard, walking past my mother and up the stairs to the big bedroom without saying a word.

Still, Eva never neglected anyone, not even the dead, and she watched her daughter more closely after that, too—until my mother gave up music and got engaged. But for all the years before Eva saw her safely married, she sent my mother to the synagogue cemetery on the anniversary of Kristallnacht to leave a vase of roses on Miss Beagle's grave. The first time Eva simply stood at the cemetery gate and pointed my mother in the right direction. After that, Eva sent her alone, knowing that even the smallest act teaches an indelible lesson. Telling me this, my mother gives a brittle laugh. "My God," she says, "I could get there even now—I could get there in my sleep." Her eyes are bright with grief as she stops talking, and I follow her in silence all the way out to the far fenceline, to the margin reserved for solitaries and suicides, far away from the family plots.

ORPHAN OF LOVE

I t was early in the morning, early spring in Indiana, bitterly cold. Imagine elm trees, a smooth gray sidewalk without cracks: exactly the kind of small-town neighborhood my father used to fantasize about when he was a kid in the Chicago slums. He'd picture his parents dead, perished in fire or flood, and himself standing on a street corner just like this, all alone with his suitcase, free to select his new family purely by the look of their house. My father, Abe Gershon, was twenty-eight years old when he stood on the Shapiros' porch in the spring of 1941, a medical resident on his first house call, but it came to him again, the brief, secret indulgence of childhood: I HEREBY CHOOSE THIS FAMILY. His belly tightened as if he hadn't eaten for days. He tugged at his pants so they'd hang right, so the lady of the house wouldn't immediately see that he had a bum leg. *(Stricken, not bum, his mother always said. Hold your head up high.*) Then, just as he raised his hand to knock, the door opened, and before him stood a housewife neatly aproned and delicately built, the opposite of his own. That's how he knew the future had arrived.

My father's last stories often began like this, with a little coincidence, a moment in which the world rose up to meet his secret wish. He lay in his hospital bed, the corners of his mouth whitened and sticky as he took a sip of water. "Just let me tell you this," he'd say. "Here's something your mother doesn't know." After he was dead she didn't deny his stories, but she didn't say they were true, either. "From what I can gather," she said bitterly, "his family had a different policy about the truth."

But what if she loved this about him when they first began? She'd have been hungry for any kind of drama after a childhood in that nice town, that neat house, with a father who couldn't end a story and a mother who refused to begin. This young doctor, on the other hand, gave his stories the bright colors, the simple lines of a Sunday schoolbook: the baby in the bulrushes rescued by a princess; the boy left in a pit for dead, only to become king of his enemies. He must have told her almost nothing true, and the one time she insisted on seeing a photo of his parents, he had nothing to say about it. I've seen this picture: did my father choose it because it gave nothing away? There is a father, slender and slope-shouldered, and a mother huge beside him, both their faces austere and unreadable like those of circus performers resting between shows. Maybe my mother felt a first little question rising then, but it would have been nothing she could put into words, and easy enough to brush away.

But this is supposed to be my father's version, my father who on his deathbed wanted to tell me a love story. He began it there, on the porch, the hero at the first enchanted door, taking a deep breath and holding out his hand to a handsome matriarch. My mother later insisted it was nothing so grand. Her father, a diabetic, had walked into a wall in the dark one night, and stubbed his big toe—the danger of infection was high.

"Dr. Gershon, from the hospital," said my father briskly. "How's the patient feeling this morning?"

He must have made a complicated first impression, this young doctor, with his slenderness, his shabby overcoat, the square small mustache like a felt patch under his nose. Slightly fraudulent, but attractively so, in Grandmother Eva's memory. The slump to the shoulders hinted at the truth: a deep and driving loneliness, a fragility at the core that drew women. She saw it, but it worked on her, anyway. She leaned toward him, lifting his name tag in two fingers.

"Jewish," she said. "Where are your people?"

"Dead," said the doctor. "Everybody dead but me."

It was a stroke of genius. "Mein Gott, what a world," she said, her face swept pale. Then she regained herself. "Please come in, Doctor, don't stand in the cold. Only be quiet going up the stairs—our Clara's a light sleeper."

WHAT EVA SAID ABOUT HER DAUGHTER wasn't true either, and she later claimed never to know why she said it. "I stand accused," she'd tell me, shrugging. But it matters, as much as my father's orphan lie, because my mother's sleeping was the dangerous thing about her. Once she went under, none of us could wake her: she went down into dreams like a spelunker, roped herself down and took the rope too, and only came up when she was good and ready. On their honeymoon, my father saw this for himself, a little truth that had been kept from him in courtship, the way other families keep secret some inherited defect or story of dishonor. Their first morning together, he awoke in the gray light to see that his wife had pulled her pillow down over her ears and was holding it there, hard. Later she assured him it was against the roaring of the Falls, but by then he already suspected the truth, that she wasn't in love with him and maybe couldn't love anyone really. He'd watched her sleep, a reasonable bridegroom thing to do, had seen her come up and out of her dreams as if she'd been on the longest train ride of her life and he was a servant sent to meet her at the station. Her face was pale blue in the morning light, a haughtiness in it he hadn't seen before. What if she wasn't the warmhearted girl she seemed in daylight? A crazy idea, but it wouldn't go away, the possibility of cruelty. This isn't something he told me, but what if it stayed with him, making him feel secretly justified years later when he stepped into his own dangerous dream of love?

But my mother was a dreamer too, and she remembered how, the morning of that first house call, my father's footstep, the way he came down heavily on his good leg, entered her life first through dream. "I've forgotten half my life," she'd say. "Why do I remember that?" In the dream, she was performing, but the music on the piano had just revealed itself to be an unknown and maniacal piece, and offstage somebody else was playing a waltz, so she was forced into a mad duet, a hectic parody of the Bach two-part invention she was preparing, in real life, for her upcoming college recital. Dragging herself awake, she still heard the off-beat heavily in her head. She was amazed later when she saw who made that sound in real life, how small and slender he was, with a comedian's sad eyebrows, and so thin she could circle his wrist with her fingers.

But not yet. By this time sunlight had reached her bed, a deceptively warm yellow light that didn't want to let her go. She listened, feeling exactly the way she did in dreams, or when playing certain piano pieces she knew by heart: in a resting state, but keenly alert to the nuances of some other language or logic. She couldn't shake the dreamer's feeling of being guided along a necessary path, even as she came awake and recalled that a doctor was expected this morning. She smiled a little, to think of the pretty sight she'd make in her nightgown, but surely something bigger, some buried desire for drama sent her toward the bedroom door, wanting consequence. She couldn't know this, at nineteen. She only knew that her hair was beautifully unkempt and that when she stepped into the hallway, sunlight would stream out with her.

So she appeared, a girl in a white nightgown and a flood of light, at the very moment the doctor gained the top of the stairs. She looked him dead in the eye, not at all demure, not even human, but pure commandment. *Go ahead and fall in love with me.*

Then she woke up to the flat facts of him, facts she'd spend months denying to herself. He was a skinny young man with a limp and a sad face. His eyes were beautifully blue, but dog-desperate, out for whatever he could get. And then there was that awful mustache. In frank dismay she put her hand to her mouth and rushed back into her bedroom.

For Abe Gershon, it didn't matter: A beautiful girl from a good family had at last appeared in his life. She was gone, vanished, but for a second he still saw the wide white fan of her nightgown curving in the light, a vision meant only for him. Then nothing but a pure empty hallway, bereft of her.

THE THRILL OF RISING ACTION, of medical crisis and the tough decision: this is what mattered in my father's telling, for even as he unwrapped the thin bandage around Jake Shapiro's big toe, he knew that the foot could not be saved and that the amputation itself might kill the patient. But underneath all this, did he also realize that the moment he hospitalized my grandfather he would lose access to the mysterious, essential thing he'd begun to crave? He must have felt suddenly that he couldn't live without this family, this girl. He needed their world: the hall hat stand, the banisters, the dark and heavy European furniture, the piano with the music so prettily, seriously opened, all of it like a painting of the life he'd always felt he was meant for, and kept from. His heart tightened painfully when he imagined Eva and the girl Clara eating supper alone after the funeral, and he caught himself again: The strength of this desire made him restless and embarrassed.

The next morning when he woke in his own dark, cramped apartment, he vowed that on this new day he would be completely professional. They must never know that suspense was devouring him, that already he'd imagined Clara paying him a visit in his apartment and being overwhelmed with pity and admiration, perhaps letting him kiss her and touch her hair. He went so far as to arrange his few knickknacks and bachelor dishes to make his loneliness look provisional, the necessary monastic phase in the ambitious life. He deliberately bathed in cold water, fought the urge to light the little gas heater, even denied himself the pleasure of a coffee and a roll at the bakery, knowing that the denial would translate into a look of hunger and sadness that might arouse Mrs. Shapiro's sympathies. He knew instinctively that the mother must be won before the daughter.

That morning when he arrived, there was on the kitchen table a cup of coffee, placed just so, with a sugar bun, a boiled egg, and a note from Eva: "Eat. You're too thin."

So from the moment he stepped over their threshold he was two people: the calm professional, and the secret hunter watching, waiting for opportunity. The house itself became a landscape to be learned, inch by inch: Eva's downstairs, with its square yellow kitchen, the quiet front parlor and dining room; and Jake's sick-room upstairs, with its stark white simplicity and the enormous purple beech pressing itself against the windows, and with the flattened, childlike form of Mr. Shapiro in the bed like a stage prop in this unfolding drama. Abe felt almost pure in this room, as if he really had no other motive than to save this man's life; yet the silver instruments in his own medical case shone with a faint air of judgment. He distracted himself by imagining the one place it had not been given to him to see: Clara's bedroom at the end of the hall, just before the lavatory. It was a mystery to be savored, his image of it elaborately Victorian, lacy, virginal. He actually averted his gaze to delay the pleasure, when he walked past her door on his way to the lavatory. It was too late when she finally let him see it, after they were engaged. She showed it to him casually, almost roughly, with no ceremony whatever, and he was overtaken by a brief, crushing disappointment. It was no Victorian dream but an ordinary girl's room of the time, with cheap magazine posters of Clark Gable and Cary Grant, textbooks and homework scattered on a plain desk, the white chenille bedspread identical to his own.

My mother, this Clara, never repeated her sunlit sleepwalker act, but she couldn't shake the dreamer's hypnotic feeling of moving steadily, blindly forward. Years later, she couldn't describe it any other way; it refused to come clear. It was as if some story under the story was trying to rise up. She only knew that in the three days that the young doctor had come to her house, the downstairs rooms had begun to take on a malevolent, alien personality, particularly the front parlor, where her piano stood. In a stifling silence, the furniture leered at her: the stiff velvet davenport, the heavy mahogany sideboard with its scrolled legs, and the antique monk's chair, which in the six-teenth century had some scandalous use Eva had once hinted at. On the sideboard was a mortar and pestle of dark blue glass that had always been there; from this object alone Clara felt a faint thrill of complicity.

But the piano, of all things, had turned against her. The yellow Schirmer volume of Bach's two- and three-part inventions had gone as mad as in her dream, this sublimely balanced piece of counterpoint her teacher had chosen, with Eva's blessing, for the recital. Why couldn't anybody else see the way the dark notes crowded together in a violent caprice, never letting a person breathe?

Maybe Eva wouldn't have been surprised to hear this, if Clara had tried to talk to her. But Eva wasn't really that kind of mother; the daughter of immigrants, she'd been raised to believe in the virtue of silence. It was supposed to make a child strong. So I imagine she herself was left in the dark, feeling as if someone had moved a favorite vase a little to the left. She'd have known only that something had altered in her domestic composition, that there was suddenly no place for her in the new symmetry of the sickroom. And she was forced, on top of everything else, to submit to Clara's sudden imitation of the ideal daughter. Did she sense some parody aimed at herself? For Clara was at last getting up on time, dressing modestly in a white blouse and dark navy skirt, her hair pulled up and back in schoolgirl barrettes, to stand across from the young doctor, so priestlike in his tunic, tenderly bathing Jake's foot. Why did the scene irritate Eva so? Even the young doctor seemed to be getting bigger and straighter-shouldered, as if the house itself were imbuing him with new powers. He was, by now, briskly in charge. When he arrived at the front door he immediately stepped in, bowed politely if hurriedly, and moved right past Eva, even past the sugar bun and coffee. "Oh, I can find my way, thank you."

Eva was right, of course—right and wrong. Clara intended no parody. I know this much about her, and about nineteen: It is enough work to quiet the dark shameful thrumming in your body, the velvet on your skin, the fingertips alive with sensation as your father lies there, possibly dying. He doesn't seem real exactly, but more of a test of your powers of concentration. The white sheet, the coverlet, his sticky lips as he opens them, oh, what will he say—for there is, with fathers, always the sense that they are about to tell you the one thing you need to know—a deep family secret, a hint for your future conduct in life, maybe just a hand laid tenderly on the head, as if in blessing. Some things don't change: how pale and small a father can be when he is dying, how he gets impossibly smaller each day, his dark eyes in their deep lavender folds rarely opening. Every once in a while he opens them and gives you a look of such deep surprise, as if you are the one keeping secrets. It takes him a whole minute sometimes to know you. "Daddy," you whisper, as you did when you were small. "What happened next?" But he shakes his head. "I wish I could remember," he says, with the plaintive, withholding smile of all his unfinished stories.

The only time Jake roused to his old self was during the house calls—of this Abe was proud. At morning and evening, a manly, companionable air entered the room. The patient lifted his head slightly, tried again to smile. "I should've looked where I was going, eh Doc?" he murmured each time, and Abe patted his arm and laughed. Meanwhile, Clara couldn't look at the doctor without feeling a terrible excitement, mixed up with gratitude for his kindness, for his comfortable authority with her father. Where had he come from? What had he lived through to be this strong? She must have wanted that life, whatever it was, and didn't dare look at him, for fear she'd give herself away. She looked at anything else: the debriding instruments, the doctor's hands as he examined and cleansed the toenail and the entire foot, clipped the nail with a single decisive stroke. She was ready to fetch basins of warm water, to fumble in his medical bag for the gauze and a tiny scalpel. She felt as if she were in training for a new life, a real, deliciously raw and gritty one. That evening, as she sat in the bedside chair watching him unwrap her father's bandage, she pictured a scene in which he asked her to please follow him into the small upstairs lavatory. There the young lame doctor would hurriedly push up her convent-blue skirt, back her up against the lavatory wall, reach swiftly and professionally around her back to undo her brassiere. Her heart was pounding; she looked at her father to steady herself.

"Damn it," said the doctor.

A fetid odor filled the room, as if a whole basket of fruit had rotted at once. She choked, and the next instant Abe Gershon's handkerchief was in her hand, the clean, slightly peppery smell of it saving her.

"I thought we could beat it," he said. "I really did."

Clara wasn't listening. She was looking at the dark yellow and violet stain on her father's big toe, the faint red streaks on the pale foot, that seem to have arrived all at once, between the hours of the doctor's visit. How was it possible? Should she have been watching? She thought of the lavatory scene and flushed hot; wildly, she wondered if she'd brought on the infection herself by her sordid desires. Absurd, of course—she wouldn't confess this fear to anyone, certainly not to me. But surely it lay beneath the surface, weaving itself through the tangled lines of her desire for ravishment and escape.

The doctor seemed so sensitive to everything she felt. "Come downstairs with me, into your mother's kitchen," he said. "You need a break, and I can give you a little job, to help out. Has your mother got oranges?"

A few minutes later she held in her hand one of Eva's last winter oranges, and Dr. Gershon stood behind her, his own hand cupping hers as she squeezed the orange's skin into a little mound and plunged a hypodermic in. A strand of sunlight came through the window, lighting the orange and their four hands in a stark vivid light: hers so pale, his darker, with the dark smooth hairs of his wrists emerging from the long white sleeves of his tunic. It took forever, this moment, long enough for her to fall in love with his hands. Small hands, but slightly square, a shape that suggested capability, authority, like those of the royal figures on cards, firmly gripping a scepter. Briskly, professionally, he let go of her. "Practice makes perfect, just like with your piano." His offhandedness was breathtaking; she ached to hear it again, to be destroyed by it.

But the doctor was worrying about his own next obstacle: how to get back upstairs with dignity. The house was terribly quiet, as if to test him. The ankle of his bum leg would click loudly all the way up the stairs, back to the sickroom and her father.

It did, but this was Abe Gershon's strange luck. She fell in love with that, too.

AFTER THE INCIDENT OF THE ORANGE, Eva vanishes out of their stories, upstaged by a slant of pale sunlight, a piece of fruit. Jake Shapiro was admitted to the hospital, his case turned over to the surgeon, and the house seemed empty without his constant, quiet presence. Eva stayed at the hospital herself most of the day, trapped in doorways, waiting rooms, straight chairs. For the first time, she was a receding figure in her daughter's life, and in those two days, Clara experienced waves of euphoria, the sudden, wild conviction that freedom was possible. She opened her bedroom window at bedtime so she could hear, in the dark, the minor notes of fast spring rain, and be awakened by first light, by mad birds, to watch the green emerging in the giant purple beech that pressed against the whole side of the house.

The doctor came to their house once more, briefly, to answer questions about the surgery and to offer what hope he could. But he was strangely formal and distant, and Clara felt a panic rising, the kind she remembered from childhood, when, after guests departed, the house fell silent, a deep, muffled, smoky silence that felt somehow permanent. She'd sob wildly; her parents could not console her. That was the feeling she had—along with the strange irrational certainty of nineteen—that if the doctor left her house now, he would never come back, and she'd be trapped with her mother in that silence for life. So while he talked to Eva, she wandered to the piano and tried a melancholy Chopin. She wanted to lure him to her like a siren, drive him into a hopeless passion, then reward him just a little. She sensed that the moment was crucial, that he had lost an important weapon: He could no longer deflate her power with a bit of instruction, a gentle sickroom admonishment. At the time she believed that in love he was an infant, that she could destroy him.

He had, however, one weapon left. As she walked him to the

kitchen door at the end of the visit, he said, "I can't ask you out while I'm on your father's case," and looked at her steadily for the first time.

"I know," she said, looking right back.

It is almost beautiful to me, and brave, the way neither of them would admit anything. They stood at the edge of Eva's domain, Clara on the top of the back steps, curving her foot seductively over the chipped concrete, my father just below her. It was as if a spell had been broken, or a new one cast, and I want to keep them there, at the exquisite edge, and tell them to be careful what they wish for. But it's too late, of course. Clara couldn't take her eyes off the doctor's hands, imagining for them a slightly alarming efficiency as she fell into fantasy, how he might remove her underclothes right there, his hands icy and swift on her tender skin. And what if her mother caught them, was wounded unto death by the sight of their violent passion?

But Eva left them alone, quite deliberately. This makes sense: he was, after all, going to make a good living as a doctor. She judged him to be a gentle, well-meaning young man, and Clara, left to her own devices, could easily do worse. And so Clara was left on her own, without props or high drama, as the doctor raised his damp palms to her face and kissed her. It was an ordinary kiss, slightly hurried and a little too moist, and this, along with the lack of audience, irritated my mother. She was seized by restlessness, a bitter disappointment rising up.

The kiss was over. She lifted herself on her toes, narrowed her eyes and smiled at him. "If I were you," she said, "I'd get rid of the mustache. It makes you look like Hitler."

MY MOTHER INSTANTLY REGRETTED IT; she always would. She felt it for life, suspended in the quiet depths of what she, too, wanted to be a love story; a single corrupt little cell too far down to reach. How is it that something so small has a way of growing? At first there'd have been just a slight souring that each of them felt, secretly, as they went about their lives. They saw each other only in the hospital corridors now, but they both felt it, the sudden tilt of romance into some other struggle, potent and unnamable. Abe felt shelved, somehow, and it was out of this that he played the aloof, distant professional, until she was forced to lean, conciliatory, his way. She stopped him in the corridor outside her father's ward.

"I didn't mean it the way it sounded," she said.

"Never mind," he replied.

"How poor are you?"

He nearly smiled, but not quite, her own father's familiar, withholding look. "Oh, you don't really want to know."

"Oh, but I do," she said breathlessly. "I do."

SHE DRESSED CAREFULLY FOR HER VISIT, in the blouse and convent-dark skirt she'd worn in the sickroom, and told Eva she was just going to run up to the college to check out the big piano. Eva, Eva: all the way to the doctor's apartment, she wasn't thinking of the doctor, but of the exhilaration of the lie, the brief, almost violent sensation of freedom. Then she was at his door, and he was opening it, and she could see inside. The apartment was not quite as squalid as she'd imagined; this vaguely disappointed her. But Abe, in his own way, had made preparations for this moment. He'd lit all his lamps and set out a teapot and two cups, and at last the details of the solitary life began to pull on her as they always did: the notion of a person choosing things for himself was beyond her experience. What she didn't know, of course, was that he was putting on a show of his own: creating a cozy bachelor scene, a select few pots and utensils neatly laid out to suggest self-sufficiency and hardihood, when in fact he took all his meals at the hospital, where the nuns felt for him a tremendous tenderness, as if he were the true invalid, and their patients all imposters. It doesn't matter; the possibility of ravishment was rising in her again; gorgeously blooming in her like a light, extending outward to the thin, ambitious young doctor bent helplessly over his teapot. Why else would she have moved toward him then, like the sleepwalking girl of that first morning, dreaming for herself the image of a girl from a life freer than her own? Such a girl would not hesitate to express herself. She came up behind him and put her hands lightly on his shoulders. That was all she had to do, and she knew it. He turned with the single swift gesture of her fantasies and put his hands on her waist. "You," he said.

"You yourself," she said with a teasing smile, and they leaned toward each other in the first natural movement they'd ever made together, leaning, leaning, their two stories in harmony at last—when there was a knock on the door.

"Can you hide?" he said. "In that closet there?" He opened the door and shoved books and shoes aside; in his haste he bumped up against the hanging clothes and everything, the whole meager display of shirts and trousers, cascaded down over his head.

At the time, my mother couldn't believe it. She tried to laugh as she got into the closet, but in their bitter middle years, when the silence of her childhood slipped into mine, it was the only story she'd tell about their courtship.

"It wasn't real life," she'd say, shrugging. "It was vaudeville."

THE VISITOR WAS OF COURSE HIS DEAD MOTHER, all two hundred pounds of her pressed into a blue-flowered shirtdress and tiny pumps. Years later, he'd struggle to sit up in bed to tell me this, his eyes briefly bright with anger, and I could see that she was the real story of his life, the one he couldn't get rid of. She showed up at his door because she had to; because she was the one person in the world who mortified him, and because what my mother didn't yet know (and Eva only faintly suspected), was that this son was a terrible worry, somehow vulnerable, always tottering on the edge of incompetence. He had a look, which Eva had noticed from the start, a brave fraudulence that was keeping him from sinking into despair: a despair that would wait for him as long as he lived, looking for a way in.

His mother shifted uncomfortably at the door. She was not yet the size she'd be when she was my grandmother, but to my father must have been big enough. The look on her face was eager, confident, as if she'd just stepped out of the kitchen and from one of her card games to check up on him, to see if he needed a drink of water, or any little thing. What was it about this mother, of all possible mothers? She had a terrible, pure physicality about her, like a big rock in the road you can't get around. He told me how, when he was small, she used to hoist him up the easiest way, around the waist. His shirt rode up to his chest, and her big arm scraped roughly across his goose-fleshed belly. She carried him thus, log-fashion, around the apartment. It made him shiver to think of it.

She'd already deposited her suitcase in the hotel downtown, she said, looking all around the room. She'd never dream of imposing. But surely he had time for a bite of lunch between patients. She winked broadly, lewdly, this uncanny mother. She'd noticed a nice restaurant by the train station—*schnitzel*, on a cardboard sign in the window, like a miracle. They wouldn't have to go out. Surprise! She had it right there in a box—and she held out the box with a magician's flourish, a box with a dark spreading stain along its rim.

"Actually, I'm expecting company, people from the hospital," he said. "Can I come to you at your hotel in a hour?"

She eyed him up and down.

"Mama—" he said. "Please don't say anything."

"I wouldn't dream of it," she said, winking again. "I'll be at the hotel when you're done."

Her coarseness astonished him, the way she slammed into the blunt ugly side of any life he might hope to have. He shut the front door and opened the closet, let Clara out. He didn't know what to expect; he braced himself for the end. But luckily there were tears in his eyes—genuine enough—as he slipped his arm around her waist. The tears must have moved her, for she shuddered against him. She sobbed once, and buried her head on his shoulder like a daughter.

"You lied," she said, "about your *family*."

"Wouldn't you, with a mother like that?" he said.

What would have happened if his mother hadn't shown up; if, in fact, she really was dead? Would there have been a luxurious slow rightness, a deepening of feeling? Could they have made love, and what sort of lovers would they have been? As it is, I imagine both of them to have been secretly relieved. My mother told me how she was raised by Eva to live in terror of "the sex act." And my father had never been with a virgin; the moment might be disastrous if rushed.

Still, he had to do something. "I can't afford a ring right now," he told her, trembling. "But my intentions are honorable."

He must have seemed so deliciously unschooled. She raised her face to his. "Sssh," she said. "It's okay." She smiled, still faintly touched by his quaint, bookish phrase.

NOT FOR YEARS WOULD THEY DISCUSS IT, my mother and father, but I think at the time she saw the lie as a mark in his favor. After all, she'd wished her own mother dead more than once, and he'd taken an incredible risk. It was oddly touching. A little worrisome, of course, but she could chalk it up to his struggle to rise in the world, the odds against him in every way: poverty, the leg ruined by polio, his slightly pathetic Jewish face. So she let it go, that hint of uncertainty that wouldn't quite show itself.

How is it that life conspires to make us rush past the moment that might illuminate our actions, that spindly root already reaching up and out to make the future? For at this precise moment the crisis my father had anticipated began. The surgery was over and Jake Shapiro was running a high fever. He was in shock, in and out of consciousness. In his brief awakenings, he had only one thing to say: "Make sure Clara plays the concert. She has to play."

Abe refused to leave Jake's side. Jake opened his eyes only for him now, and Eva twice put her hand on Abe's arm and let it rest there as if he were her own beloved son. He was, admittedly, avoiding his own mother, who was supposed to be dead but hovered at the margin of his new life, threatening to break in.

He needn't have worried. She was nobody's fool: She must have sensed that he was on the verge of some conquest, and that it would be dangerous to get in his way. Maybe she was proud of his ruthless drive, even the insult to her. Because it was only that, a certain ruthlessness, that would stave off bad luck for her boy. She was a card player, after all; she understood the necessity of keeping things close to the chest. But two can play at this game, as she was fond of saying. So she refused to tell him when she was planning to leave town.

Clara's recital was the only pure thing in all this, and Abe was grateful for it, a focus away from his mother and from the patient's ghostly shape under a sheet, the stump of his right leg raised in a harness above his white bed, his face blanched, his hands clammy and restless on the coverlet. Abe offered to chaperone Clara to and from the college concert hall, so that Eva could stay at Jake's side, *in case there is any change.* Eva pressed her lips together: did she feel a faint suspicion, an urge to refuse the doctor's offer? But Jake had opened his eyes. "Can you bring her here first? I want to see her in her dress before I die."

"Don't talk like that," said Eva. "Let them take a picture."

But Jake's eyes were wide open, in a terrible lucidity she couldn't ignore.

So it was that the next night my father found himself escorting a young woman in black silk through the hospital corridors. Her hair was swept up and back in a chignon, her eyes bright green against icy skin, a late winter beauty in April. The nuns and other doctors winked slyly at him, and he was buoyed up by pride, by the feeling that she had transformed him, too.

Eva backed away from the bed as Clara approached, and gave her a look of real fear, as if her daughter wasn't quite human but there on some dark errand.

"Why can't I see anything?" cried Jake. "Is she here?"

As Clara stepped closer, a nurse pulled the curtain around the bed, so Clara and Abe and Jake were caught inside, and Eva, in the confusion of the moment, was left out. My father felt it again: his strange sense of fortune, the coincidence only he could see.

"Mr. Shapiro," he whispered. "Your daughter's here. Can you open your eyes?"

In my father's telling, this was the climax, the moment he'd been waiting for his whole life, when the feeble king gives away his whole kingdom, his prized daughter, to the young hero from beyond the borders of the known province. That's how he would have finished the story, I'm sure. But he didn't finish; he had to close his eyes and rest. "Dad," I said, but he only lifted his hand from the coverlet, as if to put me off.

That's how it became my mother's story, my mother's ending. It has to be, because as she stood there in her beautiful dress, her own father couldn't open his eyes. At last he managed to clear his throat, weakly professorial. "You'll marry that man," he said flatly. His eyes remained closed. A minute passed. It would have looked like sleep to anyone who didn't know better.

"Is he still with us?" she whispered.

The doctor expertly took up the dead man's wrist. "Yes," he said. "Sleeping."

Abe and Clara didn't dare look at each other, but they both knew the future had been settled. The dead have so much power; why do we give it to them? I imagine Abe looking wildly away from the girl, at the hospital curtain, a pale wavery blue like a false sky closing in. She was so lovely, was what he'd always wanted. So why was he all heaviness and immobility? If Clara had just looked at him then, she might have seen his real helplessness, and that would have been a seed of truth between them. But she was stunned herself. It seemed like a judgment, the way her father kept his silence till the last moment, then decided her fate without looking at her. Still, the doctor said he was only sleeping; maybe she would wake him up and ask him again. So why was that old sensation of panic rising again? It felt different this time, a wider dark with no horizon. She told herself it was just the concert ahead of her, a bad case of stage fright. But I know what it was. It was the future: a clock ticking slowly in a handsome formal living room, a wife staring at a gold carpet, waiting for some murky truth to come clear at last.

The moment refuses to pass. I can't stop looking at my parents, wishing for them a different beginning. They seem so alone, with only their separate secrets for company, secrets that will grow the way a child does, with blood coursing along beneath the skin, carrying its invisible history of fantastic desire and ordinary betrayal. It's bound to be this way. God, how I want to change their stories before they become my own. I want to step inside that false sky and bring my parents' hands together just for a moment. I see them so clearly, trapped in there with a dead man, with a lie that I know must have seemed necessary at the time.

PORTRAIT OF MY MOTHER, WHO POSED NUDE IN WARTIME

My father was the photographer in our family, the one with a sense of occasion, and he bore this burden alone, as my mother refused to distinguish between famous moments and the rest of life. He made gallant jokes about this, calling himself the accursed husband; she was the only wife in their circle who didn't keep a family album, simply threw snapshots and mementos into an old shoebox where they went yellow and curled up. This is how we lost the late winter and spring of 1945, when he was in the Army medical corps, and she was pregnant with me. *Indiana, 1945* is our family's gap, our sole unrecorded moment. He mentioned this to her once, but she was unrepentant. "Oops," she said. "*Oops* isn't sorry," my father replied, but she said no more, only gave him a look of such mild surprise that he knew she'd never admit anything. Maybe he had his own secrets, because he dropped the subject fast. After he died she would tell me this story, but for years, all I knew was that my mother, who had never before seemed mysterious to me, could seal a piece of time like a letter and send it away.

There is, in fact, a picture from that spring—Grandma Eva must have taken it at my father's request. Early evening, and March, I'm guessing, because there's still a little snow in Eva's yard. My father would have seen the light fading as they ate their dinner, and risen swiftly from the table. "When else, when else?" he'd cry in his exulting, worried way, his hands trembling a bit as they did on even the smallest occasion, as if he still hadn't gotten over his own miraculous change of fortune. That was what he called it, so that as children we had a confused image of him as a boy in rags at a carnival booth, winning his college scholarship and our classy mother all in one night.

In the photograph he stands with his foot on the running board of a big dark car, reaching for my mother's shoulder, coaxing her into the frame. My brother Gabe, who would have been four by then, isn't in the picture—probably running wildly around the yard, already impossible to catch. So it's just the two of them: my slender, nervous father in his Army uniform, all dark with gleaming buttons, and my mother in something dark, too, with a white collar and cuffs, to make you think of Pilgrims and convent girls. Somber, stoic, just right for the year of moving back in with her mother. Was he hoping for a romantic wartime portrait? No luck: he was still in the act of pulling her in when Grandmother Eva clicked the shutter, so both of them appear a little tipped, off-balance. My mother's dress is all wrong, too. It blends into the twilight, leaving her face and the white collar and cuffs pale and detached, floating off from my father, the car, everything.

To move back into your widowed mother's house after five years of married life would be like being dragged into a different kind of dark: closet-dark, suffocating. Stepping back over that threshold, how do you hold on to your new self? You're not a daughter anymore but a woman who'd gotten sweaty in sex and later pushed a big baby into this world, making any ugly face you pleased. None of this would seem legitimate, even possible, in Grandmother Eva's house—my mother would have been instantly, purely, *daughter* again. It didn't matter that every week there was a letter on the hall table, then later, when he got as far as California, a series of postcards, each one absurdly bright, each with a beautiful blonde cradling oranges or an Indian maiden strolling the courtyard of a crumbling church. The messages themselves were terse, amazed telegrams from an impossible place: *Hard to believe we're in a war, it's so beautiful out here. Don't let Gabe grow too fast! Maybe you have some news for me? Your devoted swain, Abe.*

Your devoted swain. On the third postcard my mother must have frowned—if only he wouldn't try so hard. I picture her that spring afternoon, leaning down to hand the bright card to my brother, Eva right there watching her. It happened suddenly: boredom slipping over her like a harness, her arms and legs gone heavy, shackled by fatigue.

Eva shrugged. "There are plenty worse," she said, a remark simply meant to remind my mother that she was lucky, given the crazy world and her own impulsive nature, to have made even this mediocre marriage. But my mother instinctively pictured herself tottering on the rim of a seething pit, barely held back from falling into unimaginable disaster.

Eva took Gabe firmly by the wrist and motioned my mother up the staircase. "Go on up to your room, take a nap," she said. "I'll call you in an hour."

Sent to her room! It was as if nothing had changed—no husband, no child, no rented cottage of her own. In Eva's house, history was a door shut tight before my mother was born—her parents' early lives long since put away in that dark bristling silence called Europe. *Enough ugliness*, Eva always said. *Why would we burden a child?* Upstairs, Clara's girlhood bed had been carefully arranged ahead of time, a comfortable American bed with the sheets turned down, and a long-sleeved nightgown laid smoothly out. It never failed in this house: down she went and slept straight through to dark. Waking up, she couldn't get her bearings, confused briefly by the ghostly shape of her bridal bedroom. My God, which way am I facing—where is the wall, where the window? I imagine it as she once told me to, like an impossible homesickness, one that reaches back and back into all the known rooms of your life, until you give up and put out your hands into a swimming darkness like the one where we begin, where there is no memory yet of any place.

Where I must have been beginning. Every afternoon, in the lengthening spring light, my mother was tugged into foggy sleep. "Maybe I'm under a spell," she said to Eva.

"That's what your husband would call it," Eva said grimly. "How far along do you think you are?"

"God, Mother, I'm not," she said, though in fact her period was late—but it was always late, or early. She was sick to death of counting.

"Never mind," said Eva. "You just need to get out more."

Eva had an errand in mind, something to shake my mother out of her daze: "a mission of mercy" she called it. She herself was coming down with a cold, and my mother could just bestir herself to do one small favor. There was a new refugee couple in town, and the ladies of the Temple Sisterhood had been bringing them food and nice things. The wife was apparently quite ill—a female disease, that was the Sisterhood rumor—terrible, said Eva, but at least it was nothing contagious.

"Too bad," my mother blurted out, laughing crazily.

Eva's face blanched; she grasped my mother's arm. "Bite your tongue," she whispered. "You think God can't hear in America?"

The synagogue charity league in wartime: In the corners of the sanctuary lobby were heaped bags of shrunken oranges; rations of coffee and sugar; potatoes; tins of stewed prunes; badly-knitted mittens and baby booties; faded, battered toys. The ladies of the Sisterhood had been assigned to the handful of refugee families in town, and on a given Saturday they could be seen marching down the sidewalk—usually in pairs for moral support, since sometimes a refugee took the charitable gesture the wrong way, threw the ladies out "unceremoniously!" But then there were other times, times discussed at great length in the ladies' households afterward, elaborated on and built up and redecorated until they were dazzling emblems of American goodness suitable for children: how such-and-such a family allowed the Sisterhood ladies to enter the apartment, sat them down at a little deal table, and wept with gratitude. Some were wary: you had to hold out friendship like birdseed on your palm, and if you were lucky, one allowed you to teach a few useful phrases of English, and oh, so heartbreaking, offered in return a few words of her home tongue—provided it wasn't German. German nobody would talk. *I'll spit first,* said the refugees. This detail the ladies did not carry home to their children.

"The husband is an artist—but don't go getting ideas," Eva said to my mother. She frowned just the way she did when my mother was a teenager, to make sure my mother got the idea of duty—even fear—mixed in with the apparent romance of the errand. Then Eva went on building her careful picture. This artist, a Russian who'd been living in France, seemed almost too lucky. Such privilege isn't right, is it, when ordinary people are suffering so? A big museum in New York City had paid for his passage and taken care of everything: money for food and clothing, even paints and canvas, very hoity-toity. Nobody in the Sisterhood had heard of him, but she was willing to reserve judgment. The museum people wanted him to live in the city, of course, and he'd tried it for a year, but he'd grown tired of the noisy streets, the trash cans always banging. This, too, was where his wife's health had begun to decline. *He chose our town.* Eva's voice was hushed now. She was proud, almost maternal about the artist's decision to leave the city.

She lowered her voice even more: Mr. and Mrs. Artist haven't chosen a temple yet, she said, and at this precise juncture, she thrust a quart jar of chicken broth into my mother's hands.

"Oh no," murmured my mother.

"Chicken soup they'll understand, artist or no artist," said Eva. She wasn't finished yet, either. Into a mesh bag she dropped oranges, and two lopsided knitted caps, one slightly smaller for the invalid wife. "Childless," she said. "Maybe given the circumstances, this is for the best. I'll watch Gabe for you—go now." Eva gave her a light shove. "Hurry," she said. "Hurry back before it's dark."

OF COURSE EVERYTHING EVA SAID had the wrong effect: the more she shaped the story, the wilder the possibilities grew in my mother, her dreams floating up like dust gone gold in the light. She took alleys and side streets to get there. Hedges gleamed at her in the dusk; the back walls of familiar houses turned faintly pink. Sycamore, Linden, Birch—any of these might be the one that led to the house of the exiled artist and his wife, that new country where she had not yet been discovered. If only she could get rid of the chicken broth, still warm as she stepped forward, holding it up and out on the palm like a false beacon, a golden joke lifted up to the night. But Eva had trained her well: she was too superstitious to drop it.

Still, for the next ten minutes she was free of the papered walls and damask curtains of Eva's house, of the loud squat mantel clock and velvet sofa of the spotless front parlor forbidden to children. It was a big enough gift to look aimlessly up at the stars, at the black sky, fathomless and terrible and comforting all at once, to let the mind rove. To imagine the artist and his wife making their fabled escape from France, from Paris, though she had nothing to go on.

It would have to come from movies: rainy streets at night, heavy fur coats, hat brims pulled low. Then a fabulous ocean liner, its ship's horn trumpeting out the great announcement barely heard by the people on shore. But the truth was she didn't even know his name, let alone his work. Why was it that her mother had told her nothing? Not his name, not where he was from, not the sort of pictures he was famous for?

And she, herself—wasn't she equally to blame for failing to ask? And so, walking, she bowed her head, doomed to look the fool, an overgrown Girl Scout in front of these brilliant sophisticated people, and briefly, just for a flicker of a moment, she suspected this was what her mother intended. Was it some kind of test to see if she could stand the shock of the inevitable contrast, the sudden framing of her own life? *A little disappointment never hurts*, she could hear her mother saying afterward. *In the long run, it will make you stronger.* Even in the chill air, she felt the damp heat of future humiliation settling under her arms, in the creases of her palms.

But beneath it, already, her dreaminess was rising back up. She admitted this much to me: that while my father was away that spring she had to forcibly remind herself that she was a married woman, because she still felt like the young girl she'd been ten years before, long before she met him. Going down the sidewalk that day under the guise of missionary Girl Scout, she was in fact a fantastic spy, a secret invader, a thief coming to snatch a rare jewel from a black velvet case, and she would have gladly made a perfect idiot of herself if only she could have walked away afterward saying, *Now I know something I didn't know before.* What if it was all right to not love anyone in particular, she thought—to be a flying angel, observing everything with a single enchanted eye, no need to light any one place, or know any given name; to be, for a minute, as close to the burning stars as you were to the cooling earth?

WHEN THE PAINTER OPENED his front door, he was not wearing the paint-splattered smock and beret my mother had naively anticipated, but an old gray sweater that hung loose over his wrists. He took off his glasses, held out his hand. "I'm Lev. And you?" She felt strangely at ease, and amazed by herself, so grown-up, the hands not shaking at all. It was his face that made this possible: delicate, feline, the light green eyes narrow and uptilted like her own. It was the curly brown hair falling around the face like a woman's, not like any man's she knew—not like my father's, in other words: my father with his dark, carefully combed hair and his nervous urgency in all things, even in sex. *The first time is no picnic,* was all she would tell me for years. Now I know how it went for her, with the roar of the great Niagara Falls beyond the wedding-night window, how he tried to be gentle, but in his rush, clumsily pinned her hair under his hand. "Sorry!" he whispered. She knew she should laugh, but his face above hers was a mask, tense and furtive with need, and a sudden loneliness swept over her. She was surprised by the strength of her disappointment; it seemed to fling itself up and bang around the room like a crazy bird. "It's nothing, sweetheart," she said, still lying beneath him, her eyes filling up. *This is absurd,* she told herself, averting her face. *He must never know.*

95

At the front door, the artist was reaching out to take the chicken broth, the mesh bag with the two hats. "Angels so rarely bring chicken soup these days," he said mournfully, and my mother's face burned. Why, if he was mocking her, did he look at her so intently, as if enchanted by something that nobody else had divined? Holding the jar in the crook of his arm, he gestured her in. "A glass of tea, a cup of wine?" he said, laughing.

"I promised my mother I'd get right back—dark, I have a child."

"No—not a child!" he murmured, vaudeville and somber all at once, his gaze so direct that she instinctively held her coat tightly to her chest. She was a little afraid—not of him, exactly, but of the long stretch of the hallway behind him that seemed to pull her in with its dank smell, foreign and vaguely familiar all at once.

On his free hand, midway up the thumb, she saw a streak of incandescent blue. "That's a beautiful color," she said shakily.

"You're interested?" he said. "Listen, come back again soon. No soup necessary for admission. My wife will want to meet you. You have something of her family's look. Russian?"

"On my mother's side."

"It would make her very happy," he said. "Please."

It took her awhile to get back there again. She had to play it slow and smart with Eva. Emphasize the *landsmann* angle, the sick wife who wanted to meet her. "Oh, and Mother, you're right, it's not contagious," she said firmly, in the new tone she'd been trying out on Gabe. And then as if God really were listening, she got Eva's cold on the very day she planned to go back—and so did Gabe. "It's not that bad," she cried, but Eva insisted she stay in bed, lest she endanger the baby.

"Yes, Mother," she said, though this still didn't feel like pregnancy to her, here under her mother's roof. Surely by then I had begun to stir, to press and move against her, making her imagine me as a small nervous invader, a little like my father. She might have looked down and put her hand over me, but I kept kicking lightly, I refused to be still. Never mind—she didn't have to think about me yet. That night, was it a fever? A dream all dark red translucence and black, her mother's front parlor transformed by lurid red-shaded lamps, bordello fringe. Women passed through a beaded doorway, monumental women draped in veils and bearing dishes of ice and oil. *Lie down, dearie*, they said. "But it's my mother's best room! She'll have a fit—" she insisted as she lay down. They ran ice down her small childlike breasts, across her knobby hipbones—how on earth had she become a child again? They smoothed her down with oil, then ice again, preparing her for some ritual. Then, in her sleep, a warmth, a bloom of light below that flooded belly and thighs, toes and fingertips. She awoke damp and aching, needing to urinate. Eva stood over her, a cool dry palm on her forehead. She closed her eyes, pretending to be very, very ill.

"Thank God the fever broke," said Eva, looking at her warily. "Don't move a muscle, I'll get you a drink of water."

For days after, her skin was slippery; she couldn't get clean enough. She felt Eva watching her at breakfast, at dinner, at darkfall, giving her the worried look she'd give a cloudy pane of glass. "Do you want to tell me something?" Eva said, and my mother glanced up, giving her the first of those utterly mild, baffled looks that would later be her mystery. "Me?" she said, laughing. "God knows there's nothing to tell. Gabe's the one who has things to say. Ask him—he's fresh!"

"Don't push me," said Eva. "I'm in no mood." But my mother simply turned and smiled at Gabe—her excuse, her salvation. That day and days after, she escaped the house with him, took him out for walks in the town park, sat on a bench while he hid among the great trees he called the magic grove. His bright hair flickered at intervals, a sudden flame between the limbs, the greening of the trees. "Find me, Mama," he cried. "Come in here." One day, when she ducked under the boughs, she was surprised at how private this place was, how unsuspected. Passersby couldn't see her at all. For the first time in her life, she thought, *Maybe a secret isn't such a crime.*

That same day, on their way home, they came upon a tree whose long, fine, red needles swooped low to the ground like the long hair of a woman bending at the waist. From this tree came a rustling, then a low, urgent cry. I've gone crazy, she thought, and in answer there was an endless scurrying. A pair of gloved hands parted the veil of needles and out came a soldier and a girl, gone down the sidewalk in an instant. The tree was no less miraculous: Gabe reached out to touch it.

"Feel it, Mama," he said.

The needles were impossibly soft, like human hair. She thought instantly of Eva, how even this thought would appall her, would seem a mutinous act.

"Let's make this tree our secret," she said, with much more passion than she intended. "Not even Grandma can know."

"Our secret," Gabe repeated solemnly.

She took his hand. *If nothing else,* she thought, *I have given a child this.*

AT HIS FRONT DOOR LEV TOOK BOTH HER HANDS in his, warmly, warmly, then released them and opened his arms wide. Her heart beat lightly in her ears—in mine!—and she nearly closed her eyes. Open them fast, Mother—he only meant to help you off with your coat.

"Manya," he shouted. "Come downstairs, there's somebody to meet you." My mother's face was hot again, and she glanced away, down the street, and nearly prayed. She was somebody's wife, somebody's mother; he was obviously in love with his wife, and she, possibly, a dying woman. She knew this should be enough, but it wasn't, it wasn't.

A beautiful dying woman: when she came down the stairs, who could believe she was really ill? Maybe it was a story they'd put out to keep people from bothering them. Her hair floated dark around her pale, fine-featured face; everything about her was exact, concise, intentional, except her eyes—smoky black and deeply shadowed beneath. My mother was surprised: Manya had nothing whatever in common with her own family's tepid northern coloring. Why had Lev said that? He was the one. It was Lev who had her family's looks. This joke felt suddenly sweet, purely intimate, with no ragged edge of irony to cut her.

"Are you an artist, too?" she asked his wife boldly, and they both laughed. "Not far off at all," they said. "Come, have some tea. Tell us about yourself."

She fell easily into the role of their child that afternoon—a comfortable place, from which she could look out from her idiot desire undetected, her hands clasped neatly in her lap. They asked her to stay for dinner, and she telephoned Eva breathlessly. *I guess it's all right*, Eva said, sighing in that way that meant my mother would pay for this later. Back in their kitchen, she wanted to say crazy things to the artist and his wife: Lev and Manya, can I stay until midnight? Oh, can I live here? The smallest things made her ache with envy: the rough wooden kitchen table, the black teacups, a paring knife and three mushrooms resting beside it like a still life. She was almost dizzy, as if falling off the careful story her mother had built, and into a wish so fierce it might blind her.

Did they sense this? Her hunger for whatever might happen next? Because she realized that they'd both gone quiet, as if they were watching the moment slowly, luxuriantly expanding into some new shape. The three of them waited in the quiet afternoon, watching a fly buzz and land on the table, buzz and depart. It was Manya who broke the silence, turning to Lev. "You remember the one you wanted to try last fall?" She turned to my mother. "He wanted me to pose for an odalisque—what an idea! I'm worn out, and why pretend, my body is not nice anymore, not nice." She leaned forward. "Though I have a feeling about you. As if you could"—she broke off with a laugh—"but no. You are very nervous, a cautious girl. I can see exactly how you were raised. It's not your fault."

My mother sat still, her hand resting on her belly under the table. She had never been less nervous in her life—what did Manya mean? She hated that, being summed up with such confidence by a stranger! But a dreamer's stunned calm was still on her, a pure amazement at being in this kitchen, in this house; nothing could break its beauty, nothing. Lev, too, seemed caught by it. He was watching Manya carefully, as if by moving too soon, he might shatter the moment.

"I'm all right," my mother said. "I've never posed, I mean. But if you—" She felt absurdly slow, as if trying to form correct phrases in a foreign tongue. An odalisque! She'd seen these in art books: a nude lightly veiled or not at all, reclining on her dark couch, a gold necklace at the throat, a flower in the hair, nothing else. She looked at Lev. "Will Manya stay in the room? Because if my mother ever—"

At this, Lev broke into laughter and reached out for Manya's hand. "You're right—a maiden to the bitter end," he said, and sat up straight, rubbing his eyes and looking at both of them admiringly, as if he'd come out of some long, magic slumber. "Don't worry. She'll stay. And you can be sure no one will ever recognize you."

It was Manya who took charge, who guided my mother into their front room where the afternoon light would last longest, and pointed out the painted Japanese screen behind which she might disrobe—that is, if she still felt comfortable with the idea. "Of course," said my mother lightly, looking demurely down.

That day, dusk did not pull her down into sleep—not right

away. She had time to notice the bright canvases stacked against the walls, the books in precarious piles on either side of a long, blue velvet couch, the jars of brushes and vivid smears of paint, the acrid smell of solvent; to notice, before she slipped behind the Japanese screen, what was painted there: the ocean, a tree yearning its way, three women with parasols gazing back at her—surely it meant something, but she would never know what. It was strangely comforting, a mystery poised and coolly watching her till the end of time. At her feet lay a box heaped with velvet ribbons, jewels, a bunch of silk violets. "Anything you see here that you like," Manya said. My mother's flesh went suddenly cool, as if she'd stepped behind a doctor's screen, but Manya handed her a bright silk kimono. "Take your time. Lie down on this couch and call us when you're ready."

She chose bravely: a tiny golden fan, the bunch of violets— nothing that would clothe or hide her.

When they came back, and saw her lying down in the kimono with the violets and the fan, they stood perfectly still a moment, then burst into applause, a light, comical applause that made her feel safe and powerful, as if she were far away from them on a high stage. But in Lev, did she permit herself to see something more, a nod, a collusive smile as if to say, *You are beautiful, just right*, without in the least being disloyal to his wife? They were all three like tightrope walkers, she thought, playing even the smallest moment for its grace and danger. "I feel like I'm in the circus," she said, and Lev looked at her blankly, nearly frowned, by which she knew she'd surprised him, gone a little further than expected. "You'll like this, then," he said softly. "All our props are stolen.

Manya here has committed the sin of raiding your own beloved Majestic. We won't tell if you don't tell."

Manya laughed bitterly. "Here's how I'll go down in history: His wife, at the end revealed to be a chronic kleptomaniac, nearly shattered his career by stealing from small-town theaters—"

"Manya, slow down," said Lev. "You'll scare our novice."

He knelt down then, and arranged my mother. She felt her own stillness like a triumph, this new talent, the way this man couldn't see or hear or know the light double pulse beating in her veins, the twinning of my life and her excitement, a dark, sweet invasion. She refused to tremble for him, even when he leaned closer and put the bunch of violets into her other hand and with intolerable tenderness draped her elbow against her hip so the flowers fell lightly against the dark triangle of her pubic hair. The fan she was to hold over her head, he said, looking right at her. *Think of a Spanish dancer with her castanets.* "I am," she imagined herself saying, straight out of the fantastic silence of her skin, her secret in the world.

"Very chaste," he said. "Manya?"

Manya came forward and pushed the kimono lightly, roughly, back off my mother's shoulders.

Manya. Now my mother trembled, because Manya was looking straight into her, and her dark eyes knew. Did Lev? She couldn't tell; he only frowned, a workmanlike impatience sheathing his face.

"Let's get started," he said. "A fast sketch is all I need, and we'll send you home to your mama." And with a sharp look to her, he stood up and kissed Manya, light and slow on the mouth.

My mother did not faint. She was light and heat, a pure current of fury and desire. She held herself perfectly still.

"Magnificent," he said. "Manya, you've got an eye."

WHEN IN THAT HOUR DID SHE BEGIN TO FALTER, her fingers gone numb on the gold fan, sleep coming for her as it had to? And what, in an artist's front room, with its lush disorder of jumbled books and phonograph and bright paintings stacked against the walls, what in all this could have reminded her of her mother's squat mantel clock ticking in the front parlor's dark, clean silence, the forbidden velvet sofa she once lay on as a child when her parents were out; where now she pictured my bright-haired brother lying on his belly, angrily kicking his legs? *Where's Mama? I won't go to bed, I won't, till she comes. You can't make me.* Even my father appeared to her as she lay in her pose. She pictured him in a train compartment, alone and in civilian clothes, his head nodding forward as he fell asleep, too, his slender hands for once not shaking, though tightly gripping the armrests as the train hurtled toward home, vulnerable. She was startled by a sudden sweet dinging, a light endless chiming of a clock she couldn't see. On and on it went, she could swear, nine times—or more than that! She glanced up in a panic, and strangely, her gaze fell not on Lev working at his easel, but on Manya beside him, reading in a chair. How long does it take to see the simple, terrible thing? Because gradually she noticed that the collar of Manya's blouse was damp, that Manya's fingers, under lamplight, shone on the pages of the book.

"Please, no—you're crying," my mother said. "I'll leave."

"My fault completely," said Manya, standing up. "You've been a good girl. But I, for one, am off to bed. And don't anybody try to tuck me in."

Manya stood up and walked past Lev without looking at him, but just in front of my mother she slowed down, then leaned over her. "How did I miss it before?" she said. And she reached out to touch my mother's abdomen. My mother flinched, her breath knocked away by the touch of cold fingers. "Lev," said Manya. "Lev, you won't believe. Stop a minute." But Lev did not stop. My mother heard the scratch of his pencil, his steady breathing; he didn't care what became of her, or who she was in real life. And Manya—what about Manya, who was about to leave the room. Clara forced herself to look again at Manya's pale face, her reddened eyelids, and to show that she was brave, my mother took a deep breath, very deliberately so Manya would hear, and submitted, while Manya's fingertips traveled across her belly.

"Isn't it funny," Manya said. "The very place that's killing me." She turned back to Lev. "Make it stark white," she said, "so it hurts the eye to look there. God, I wish there were a color in the world like that." Then she stood up and walked out of the room.

"Wait," cried my mother, but Manya was gone, and still Lev worked. In the awkward quiet she saw her own smooth flesh white and exposed and avid—there was too much of it, a whole country of it swamping the room, alive and crude and insulting. She stood up suddenly, pulling the kimono up with her, wrapping herself in it tightly.

"Pardon, but what did you do with my clothes?" she said haughtily.

Lev sighed and put down his pencil. "Don't worry," he said calmly, as if he'd known from the beginning how it would go. "We never steal clothes. You can change behind the screen and let yourself out when you want. But you should see the sketch before you go. You might be sorry later—"

"No, thank you, I don't need to see it," she said stonily. She gathered up her clothes from behind the screen—even this felt like an important refusal—and rushed out of the room. But where to go? The rest of their house had long since gone dark. She had no idea where to go. She fumbled through a short hallway, her hands blind on the walls, until she found a door and waved her hands high in the air for a light-chain. There—it was their bathroom, the linoleum a ghastly mustard yellow, the bar of soap streaked with dirt and paint. She got herself dressed, the desolate little bulb above her head illuminating every mole and crease of her belly and thighs, the darkened aureoles of her breasts.

When she came out, she saw that she was near their kitchen, and that Manya sat at the table again, her shoulders curving forward, her head down. The rest of their house was a maze to my mother now; she felt she had no choice but to go to Manya and ask the way out. But when she got there, Lev sat across from her on the other side of the table, both his hands stretched across to hold Manya's. She needn't have worried: as she came forward, neither of them looked up. The black teacups were still on the table, the mushrooms on the breadboard, flat gray and stale under the harsh, ordinary kitchen light. A still life, she thought again, only nobody would want to paint it.

"Goodbye," she said, and without waiting to see if they'd

looked up, she opened their back door and stumbled out onto a porch. Once down, she moved her hands along what felt in the dark like a rough, wild mass of hedge, until she came at last to cold metal, a garden gate she hadn't known was there. She lifted the latch and let herself out onto the sidewalk, her own town, a strangely warm and noisy night. Noisy—why? It was May, early May—there was no holiday then that she knew of. But car horns honked; firecrackers sputtered from the direction of downtown. *Who do they think they are?* she thought wildly. *Idiots— it's not any holiday.*

EVA WAS WAITING FOR HER AT THE FRONT DOOR, of course, her arms folded across her chest in her habitual posture of forbearance, but strangely, there was no recrimination in her eyes, only a deep weariness that haunted my mother as she walked past her, going in.

"Gabe?" asked my mother.

"Awake," said Eva. "I wash my hands. And by the way, your husband's home, upstairs and waiting. He wanted to surprise you."

My mother said nothing, but went slowly toward the stairs. It was all as she'd known it would be: she looked into the parlor and saw Gabe exactly where she'd imagined him, on the forbidden sofa, crying and kicking his legs, refusing to look her in the eye. And the radio was on, as it never was late at night in Eva's house— a jumble of band music and excited voices, static, then strangely, a woman sobbing as she tried to speak through the jubilation.

"Mother, tell me what's happened," she cried. "Has something changed?"

"Only the whole world," said Eva, sighing. "What could it possibly matter to you?"

IN ALL THE YEARS OF OUR CHILDHOOD, my mother made sure my brother and I were never late for a big occasion. If we had somewhere to go—a wedding, a funeral, a formal gathering of any kind—she stood in our bedroom doorways and tapped her foot, or pleaded from the foot of the stairs, "Can't we be on time? Just this once?" Not even my father, who wanted so badly for the world to see his family whole and right, could match this panic of hers. She was never comfortable at big parties and celebrations—*ordeals*, she called them—but when the time came, she hurried us into the car so fast our hearts pounded wildly. "It matters to me," was all she'd say.

It took years, and my father's death, for her panic to fade, for her to begin to tell me things. But she would never tell me Lev's real name, or if the painting was somewhere I could find it. "I wish I knew," she told me once, in her exasperatingly mild, indifferent tone. "I don't know if he even finished it. If he did, he took it away with him when his wife died." She looked at me with pure astonishment, as if she were still a naive young woman, and all of this had just happened. "What matters is that Manya was dying," she said to me. She closed her eyes and took a deep breath. "I'm sorry. Say anything you want, but no piece of art can make up for that, ever."

NOT HIS LAST NAME, not the name of the painting, but the rest of the story—this she would tell, blandly, dully, as if she were pulling heavy curtains across a theater stage. "It was over, everything at once," she said. A month after the armistice and a week after his wife's death, Lev sent a thank-you note to the temple: they'd taken care of Manya's cremation for him, no charge, and they would be so honored if he'd let them keep the urn with her ashes there, in their own Jewish cemetery. They would even donate a handsome engraved plaque for the memorial wall. He must have slipped the note under the door in the night—nobody saw him deliver it. No thank you, he wrote, *You've been too generous already. She's coming with me.* And then one day, without warning, he was gone—with Manya's urn, his suitcases, the big canvases, boxes, and jars. Nobody knew where he'd gone, though briefly there was speculation: back to New York, or maybe all the way to Paris. Wasn't that where all the big-shot artistic types went when they were finished using up America's little towns?

But this bitterness didn't last long. Amidst the crazy jubilation of boys coming home and the plain fact of a husband's bereavement, who could sustain hard feelings? Never mind—let history move forward again, carrying my mother along with it. History in the shape of my father, tanned and triumphant, and not empty-handed either—he'd come back with a bundle of brightly colored real-estate brochures and a quiet new confidence. Even that first night she saw it. He didn't ask her where she'd been but simply held her in a tender, certain embrace in her girlhood bed, holding before her the brochures with their scenes of California's spectacular coastline, its abundant valleys—spreading them before her as if she were his child, and this, a bedtime story. She leaned back into him; it was easy, comforting. "The fruited plains," he said. "For once they're not lying. What do you say—westward ho?"

He lay his hand on her belly then and leaned down, smiling. "Let's get you out of this trap," he whispered, and wildly she thought, *My God, which one of us does he mean?* She smiled for him, granting him his witty moment, but he took this to mean she was willing to make love and moved his hand smoothly, smoothly, down toward her sex. She flinched. "Oh, Sweetie," she said, working a little shakiness into her voice. "Can you wait, can you give me a night to get used to—"

"It's the baby, isn't it?" he said tenderly, innocently, and she bowed her head in gratitude.

"Tomorrow night," she said. "I promise."

SURELY SHE KNEW LEV'S REAL NAME, his whole name; surely she knew enough about the painting to recognize it later. What if it is in one of her old art-history books, on my own bookshelf now, in plain view and utterly hidden?

"Forget the painting, remember Manya," she said to me. I was grown by then, and she was very ill. Her eyes, as she finished the story, were as dark and deeply shadowed as Manya's must have been.

"Forget the painting," she said to me. If I can't, it's because of that moment just before she fled, the moment Lev finally put down his pencil and asked her if she wanted—no, *needed*—to see the sketch before she left. "No," she cried.

No? From everything she told me, I don't believe her. I know

Lev to have been quick in all things, a little wild—maybe not unlike her. Maybe he knew something about the dark undiscovered spring at the heart of her, knew that later she would wish, just as fervently, that she had said yes. What else could he offer her, how else to say it? He turned the easel around.

Here you aren't, he could have said tenderly, in a voice with no mockery at all, a voice that would give her a gift even as it pretended to deny her. So that she saw, before she ran away, her own hand languidly covering her sex with a bunch of flowers, and her own pale torso transformed. It was true, Mother, you were no longer yourself, but an angel floating in a depth of blue, your eyes pure and austere with years of watching, your body skimming the air.

Later that night you would lie with my father, his hands and yours pressed together over the place where I fed and grew, where other cells, inevitably, would one day feed and divide. You closed your eyes so he wouldn't see you crying, wouldn't see your guilt and confusion, your panic as you tried to picture the future, and couldn't—that way was dark too. It's late, Mother, but listen anyway, while I tell my children that somewhere in the world there is a painting of you and me, and in that painting your womb is not stark white and humanly cursed, but a whole dazzling universe, the burning blue-white of bones and stars.

THE HANDCUFF KING

On the big trip west, the backseat of the Pontiac was my brother's secret world, a dark canyon mapped with cracks and sweating like skin. He watched the dust angels rise and fall for hours, floating with them in a narrow brown world our parents knew nothing about, the creased cliffs and sullen valleys where he was sometimes prisoner, sometimes king, but always, always, escaping. Beside him slept the new dog, the black spaniel our father had bought to help with the big move, and later, my arrival. But nothing could stop Father from worrying: whenever he turned around to look at Gabe, he saw the same glazed look, utterly vacant. Was damage being done, somehow, by their moving? They'd invited Gabe to name the dog himself, but so far, he'd said nothing.

"A few days from now you'll see the ocean," Father said.

"How does that sound?" Gabe nodded politely. He was exactly five. Time was a field fanning open, then closed, a black road dissolving in the sky.

Nobody had spoken, it seemed, for days. And then:

"Let's call her Longo," said Gabe.

"That's a funny name, a fine name," said Father. "But maybe Spot would be easier, or Prince?"

"Longo," Gabe repeated. A beautiful blue marble in the mouth. "Longo," he whispered. "Thou shalt not do blongdonimo on the seat."

The only other time Gabe came to life was when they stopped at a roadside park, a gas station. But in this, too, he was uncanny. "Hi," he'd cry out, lassoing perfect strangers if they got close. "My daddy fought Hitler in California, and real estate is the way to go." Everybody smiled. "Smart kid, how old is he?" they'd say, then stand there, as if waiting for more. It didn't matter who: gas-station men and waitresses, storekeepers and soldiers traveling home, whole families having picnics next to their cars—Gabe arrested them all. "I'm five and a quarter," he'd tell them, but still they waited.

"And I'm 4-F," my father would add, pointing to his bum leg. "Served in the Zone of Interior. I wanted to fight, God knows."

People were sympathetic, if shy: hands shoved in coat pockets, eyes cast to the far distance. "Roosevelt himself," some-one might murmur, and for a minute, he was absolved.

Back in the car. Endless fans of yellow grass, our parents' necks perfectly rigid, unmoving. Father's was tanned and creased, Mother's pale below the edge of her silky scarf. The difference seemed to matter.

Father cleared his throat. "Kansas," he said. "We're making progress."

All the words of that trip must have hissed, tall and thin like the grass outside. Is that where *Longo* came from, so starkly opposite? He wanted to ask Mother if it was California yet, but how could he when she sat so still, her neck white, the scarf alive against it. She kept the road-book on her lap, way up high now, because the baby took up so much room. "Don't worry," she'd told him. "It won't happen till we get to California—God willing," and laughed in a new, broken-off way.

Maybe it was the baby's fault. *Baby, California,* neither one was real to him. When they'd left Grandma Eva's house, she'd told him to be careful, that California was on a tilt, and that frankly, this move was one of his father's less intelligent schemes. "Just between us," she said, making Gabe feel heavy and sad inside, as if she'd handed him something to carry and not show anyone. But the tilt gave him hope. You couldn't see it in the pictures they'd shown him, but he believed in it anyway. It made more sense than the pictures, where mountains rose straight up out of fields. Already the young scientist, my brother, full of healthy mistrust. He was ready for the tilt to start right now, a slant leading straight to a big rocky wall you could put your hands against. Push and push, it wouldn't budge. Not like this place, with its flat pale fields going by fast, and sometimes a tower of grass standing up by itself, surrounded by nothing, held together by nothing.

———

AT DUSK, A WARM SMOTHERY SMELL came off the fields, just like at home, a summer night on Grandma Eva's porch. She'd shake her head and say, "They never let you forget you're in a cow town, do they?"

Mother made a low quiet noise in her throat. "God, that smell—Abe, I need to stop," she said, and Gabe's own stomach flared hot. Could a smell secretly follow you, and pop up later, cruelly? He remembered the way Grandma Eva bent down to kiss him goodbye, whispering, "Just between you and me." Mother and Father were already in the car, Mother tying on her scarf. Gabe had jerked away from Grandma a little, and she'd started to cry. In his head, a little chorus sang out, "You made her cry, you made her cry."

But as they left, Mother smiled. Had he made that happen too?

"Goodbye Mom, Goodbye Indiana," she'd called out, waving slowly, a queen in a parade.

"You'll be happier," Father had said to her. "The ocean is this amazing blue, and the orange trees give off this fantastic perfume, not like this place—"

"I thought you were in a war out there?"

"Clara. I'll try if you try."

"You try first," she'd said, and gone quiet again.

ALREADY OUR PARENTS KEPT SECRETS. And already, at five, Gabe knew it. He absorbed what he could, taking what he saw and heard and knew, in that way nobody can explain but is real, nonetheless. He took it quietly inside, as far as it could possibly go. He was going to hold onto everything from now on: what people said and what they didn't, the way they told stories, the different music of secrets. He was ready that night, in the motel room, when Mother turned to him and said, "Gabe, I'll tell you a story. Not about us. This is from long ago, another time and place."

That night's room was no different than the one before. Twin beds and a narrow cot on wheels, long heavy orange curtains, a peppery smell that would, his whole life, make him feel suddenly empty, deflated, *gone*: as if his life were over. It felt true, absolute, he could never say why. At twenty-eight, on a field trip with other graduate students, or at forty, traveling with his own wife and child, it wouldn't matter. He'd smell it, and his stomach would clench. "It's nothing—just me," he'd say, waiting to come back to life.

But that night, Father was already asleep on one bed, the dog at his feet, its round belly pumping fast, even in sleep. On the other, Mother waited, patting a place beside her. In her quilted blue robe, her hair piled high on her head, she was a queen again, a ballerina on a circus horse.

"This is about a boy who loved the smallest places, the places everybody else called traps," she said. "Jails and water tanks, cages and coffins, the deepest caves. He was famous for escaping them, but the truth was, that was just to keep his audience happy. What really pleased him was the waiting that came before, the private world nobody knew he had, when he had time to look long and hard at the two faces in a single stone, the maze in his own thumbprint, the silver bubbles rising up before he did—"

"That's about me," he said. "I'm the boy."

She lay her hand on his head, and though she didn't answer, he felt briefly warm, safe. But just as he caught the scent of her lotion, *her* smell, she slipped her hand away, turned it palm down, and frowned. "What if I dry up out there?" she said, with the broken-off laugh, and he watched her closely. Her hands rose up and fluttered back down to her lap. "This boy," she said, "could stay hours in such places, discovering the smallest things. Only at the last minute would he glance at his watch and wriggle up and out. He had great strength, he was slippery as a snake, but it was his amazing concentration that was the real magic. Do you know what they called him in my day? The Jewish Handcuff King."

He realized, sleepily, that he wasn't the boy she was talking about. Then the bedspread was empty, dented, and she was standing by the window, grasping the big orange drapes in her hands.

"Mama, what was his name in real life?"

"You sound like a grown-up already," she said. "It's funny, how early we start to need answers—"

"Are you two still awake?" said Father, propping himself up on one elbow, and looking at her with his eyebrows raised. "Wouldn't he be better off with *Robin Hood*, maybe *Jack and the Beanstalk?*"

"I'm not so sure," she said. "But go ahead, tell him a story."

"I would, but the driving's got me beat." He sighed and turned over, his back curved and small under the sheet. That was another thing Gabe saw: that at night Father shrank, and Mother got taller. On the bed Father looked small, the hair on his forearms and the backs of his pale hands as silky dark as the dog's fur. He'd kicked off the covers, showing his bad foot, the one curved and small, the skinny ankle not much bigger than Gabe's own. *The bad foot*—Father's own name for it—hung over the edge of the bed now, like a thing to be kept separate. How could Father fall asleep so fast, when Mother stood there, the baby making her lean forward, too close to the window.

But he wasn't asleep after all. "Clara, sweetheart, close the drapes," he said. "The whole world can see in."

IN THE MORNING, IT WAS FATHER who stood at the window, pulling the curtains sharply back. Sunlight fell on the beds in a bright swath, turning the dog blue-black and Mother stark white. She lay on her back, her hands resting on her stomach. "It's some kind of luck," she said. "I must have done something in a former life."

"It's what we want, isn't it?" said Father. "So we goofed on the timing."

"We?" she said. "Abe, please."

For a long moment, nothing happened. There was no car outside, no dog, no California. She'd stopped time. It was Father who started it again: buttoning his shirt, flexing his wrists to button the cuff buttons. His wrist, under the silver wristwatch, was dark and powerful now. Gabe kept his eye on it, even when they went outside to let the dog relieve herself on the grass. Still holding the leash in one hand, Father opened his big guidebook, and hunkered down beside Gabe. "Your mama's adjusting to the baby, that's all. It takes awhile with some mothers, but it's okay. Listen, why don't you tell me about California, what you know so far."

"Poppies," Gabe said. "And the hurt castle."

"The hurt castle, very good!" Father laughed. Then he sighed and tapped his watch. "Okay, pop into the car, and the dog, too: let's surprise your mother, everybody will be ready to go when she comes out."

How did it start? As a flickering match-flame in the arms and wrists, as Gabe looked up at Father's tanned arms, with their smooth hairs all running one way, his wristwatch, his billowy white shirt. Father suddenly took up too much room in the world, and the little chorus cried "Run, Gabe, run!" and he couldn't stop himself. For a split second that's all there was to it: sweet tangy air, a wild happiness, then he knew he had to run *somewhere*. And there was the dog, hunched awkwardly on the grass, her neck craning around as he rushed toward her, grasped her hard around her ribs. He squeezed her until she wheeled on him, her teeth and gums showing.

"For God's sake," cried Father, pulling the dog sharply up by the collar. He knelt beside Gabe, held him hard. "What got into you? Don't you like the doggy?"

"I don't know," said Gabe. "You can let go of me now." Somehow Father was the right size again, and the chorus, satisfied, had disappeared.

AT NOON THERE WAS A STONE WALL, and a stone stairway to climb, up to the top of a bluff. Father shaded his eyes and planted his good leg up on a narrow ledge, exactly like the figures on the big plaque, except that the wind whipped so hard at his pants, Gabe worried that he might come loose, get carried off the bluff. "Thar she blows," Father said, lifting him onto the ledge. A slip of muddy green water hung just beyond the trees. "William Becknell, Father of the Sante Fe Trail. On this spot he split open his saddlebags and Spanish gold fell to the ground in heaps. Sounds like a song, *Spanish Gold.* In California, there were wonderful songs like that."

Mother smiled at the muddy green. "Was there a lot of good music in California?" She held up the guidebook and dangled it over the bluff. "Speaking of fathers, listen to the names of these towns: Alexander, Albert, Otis, Odin. Oh, and Lorraine! A lone Lorraine way out here."

"Clara, you seem wound up."

"I won't say another word."

"You're exhausted, I know. We'll stop early tonight, how about?"

She shrugged. "Do what's best for Gabe," she said. "This has got to be tough on him."

"Gabe's fine. Gabe's a trooper," Father said. "Aren't you?"

"I guess," Gabe said, but the wind carried that off, too.

IN THE DUSK, ONLY THEIR HEADS and the backs of their necks still showed: Father's was already fading, his hair just a shadow above his collar. Mother's, under the yellow scarf, was ghost-white, with a streak of sunburn like a tiny brand. Gabe watched the streak carefully; it would be the next to go.

121

"This time I definitely need to stop," she said.

"I think we're almost to something," Father said. "Can you hang on just a bit longer?"

"No," she said. "Now."

He pulled over fast, and she got out of the car, walked off into the dark field.

"You don't have to walk a hundred miles," cried Father, but she kept on walking until she was just a stick of white and Gabe had to squint to see her. She got small, smaller.

"Mama," he cried.

"She's okay, son," said Father. "She just needs a minute."

But the world had gone quiet without her. Quiet and huge and alive in the wrong way. Even when she got back in and Father started the engine again. Bundles of yellow weeds leapt up beside the car, fell under the wheels, got dragged along. A deer held still in the road and stared at them until at last Father stopped. "What's this?" said Father. "A deer with a death wish?"

"Maybe it's a doe," said Mother.

"What's a doe," asked Gabe, but they still couldn't hear him, and that was all anybody said, for what felt like hours. Mother was sleeping, or maybe playing possum, but her scarf flapped against her neck the way it would on a scarecrow, on nothing alive. The sky deepened every minute—there was no stopping it. A rim of lights came out on the horizon, then the horizon itself disappeared. Out of the grass a bird surged straight up, its wings beating too fast to see.

"Gabe, son, are you awake? Can you hear this?" whispered Father. On the radio, under scratchy static, a man was talking fast, in a singing voice, pure and weightless. Every once in a while he said a word Gabe recognized—*basketball, hamburger, America*—and these words sounded heavier than the rest. They pulled on the man's voice and dragged it down. Gabe wished there wouldn't be any words he knew. They didn't belong in the beautiful rush of sound.

"That's Spanish, son. Isn't it pretty?"

Gabe nodded. The rushing voice soothed his belly.

"Land of the piñon pine," said Father. "Tomorrow morning, you'll see the color of the dirt here, almost pink. From here on out, everything looks different."

Already that was true. On the horizon, swollen black clouds were stacked up in a long row, a clear gold light streaming out beneath. The road shone, and Gabe didn't mind Mother's silence now: this was something he could look at a long time. Then they were on a wide street with flat-roofed buildings. A restaurant, a gas station, a saloon with double doors. Bright tall letters, a wagon wheel, a red horse bucking in the violet sky.

"You can decide where we stay tonight," said Father.

Gabe chose the tallest, brightest sign: the green-red-yellow head of an Indian chief.

"The Chief it is," said Father. "God, I can almost breathe out here."

SHOULDN'T THE ROOM HAVE LOOKED DIFFERENT? Shouldn't it have had rough log walls like a pioneer cabin, lanterns, all golden, to see by? It was just like all the others: two beds, the dull orange curtains, the peppery smell. A man shoved a folding cot through the door and opened it between the beds. "The dog is our only problem," he said. "I'm sorry—the dog is cute but it will have to stay in the car."

"Don't worry," whispered Father. "We'll sneak her in after dark."

After the man was gone, Mother shook her head. "Why do they make the cots so narrow? The slightest move, and he'll fall out."

Her voice surprised Gabe: how long had it been since she'd said anything? But Father was already busy, taking the pillows from the beds, banking them around the cot.

"Thank you," she said. "I'm sorry. Am I being unreasonable?"

"No," said Father. "You're not unreasonable at all. And I'm sorry—"

"Ssh," she said, smiling at Gabe. "It can wait. And I mean it. Thank you."

On the wall right over the cot, was a portrait of an Indian— the Chief himself? He looked straight into Gabe's eyes, frowning under his heavy headdress.

Father was checking the guidebook. "Somewhere near here there was a massacre."

"Can we wait on the massacre?" said Mother. "I don't want to be a wet blanket, but—"

She sat down on one of the beds and plucked at the spread, dull orange like the curtains. "Gabe," she said. "Let's go back to that story, the Jewish Handcuff King, Mr. Harry Houdini. You wanted to know his real name, and I'll tell you. It was Harry Weiss. Not very dramatic, so he changed it. But listen, when he was eight years old he moved on from card tricks and handkerchiefs to locks. He could pick any lock, and learned to make tiny skeleton keys which he hid on his body. Once, near the end of his life, he was locked in a Russian prison cell without his tools. The witnesses held their breath and the prison guards gloated: this time they had him! But do you know, at that moment he made a last request, that his wife be allowed to give him a farewell kiss. And what did she do but pass him, in that kiss, a perfect tiny key."

"Clara," said Father. "Not to quibble, but is this better than a massacre, story-wise?"

"Absolutely," she said. "There's hardly anything to it, so tender and smart and subtle. Although not long after this, he got kicked in the stomach during a performance, I don't know by what—a horse, a donkey, but I can imagine the bellyache, can't you? He kept right on performing, got himself out of whatever he'd been paid to get into, and took his bow."

She stopped talking and leaned back, her chin tilted up, eyelids closed. "Sorry, got dizzy," she said. "Where were we?"

"He got kicked," Gabe said.

She shook her head.

"Daddy, can you finish it?"

"I wouldn't dare," said Father. "Besides which, I don't know how it ends."

"I saw a restaurant on the way in," she said. "Why don't you boys go on without me."

"You could at least sit with us," said Father. "Maybe soup would go down. We could be like a real family."

"I've got news for you," she said softly. "We are a real family."

She touched Father's hand and Father looked at her, wouldn't stop looking at her. Gabe wanted them to stay like that, but the instant he thought it, she took her hand away.

"Trust me," she said. "Just go."

FROM THE OUTSIDE THE RESTAURANT GLOWED yellow and warm under its dark roof. People leaned toward each other, their heads haloed under the lights. There were red-checked tablecloths, red leather booths, and elk heads on the wall, their eyes gazing down.

"This looks promising," said Father, once they were sitting down.

"Finish it now," said Gabe. "The story."

"Son, give it a rest."

"I want to know about Harry Weiss," Gabe said. "I want to know what happened next."

"Why don't I tell you a real one instead?" said Father. "You're going to have a brother or sister pretty soon, and when your mother's carrying, she gets a little sad. If she seems strange, don't worry about it. She'll be better in no time at all."

Gabe waited. This was not the right story, and he could feel sentences piling up, whole strings of them. When at last the waitress brought their food, Father studied his plate, then looked at Gabe, putting one hand out across the table. Gabe couldn't think of another way to ask about Harry Weiss.

"Eat," said Father. "God, I sound like your grandma."

"Why is Mama sick?"

"I told you. The baby. Please eat, just a little."

"I'm sick too," Gabe said firmly.

Father put down his fork. His hands trembled, and Gabe waited for something to happen. But Father only took out his wallet, his fingers still shaking as he grasped the bills. He stood up, lifted Gabe out of the booth, and didn't say another word until they were outside the bright windows, looking in once again. He squatted down low the way he had outside the motel, down at Gabe's eye level. "Listen, son, maybe I'm no prince. Maybe I'm never going to be a famous professor, or a musician— though why it's not enough I'm a medical man, I'll never know." He sighed. "Who am I talking to? I'm crazy. Let's get you an ice cream, then go back and see how she is."

It was better with Father this way, just walking together, not having to learn things. They passed a park, a set of gas tanks. Against the black sky a small low building with a glass front was lit up inside, so they could see everything: three caged windows, a row of empty chairs, and a woman, standing absolutely still under the big chalkboard, gazing up as if she'd been touched in a game of statues.

Father's hand was on his arm, then on his shoulder, warm and tight.

"Look, there's Mama," Gabe said.

"No," said Father, pulling him along. "That lady's not pregnant, see? Come on."

"I want to go back," Gabe said.

"It's not her."

But Gabe had closed his eyes, and was trying to picture their room at the Chief, trying to picture Mother in one of the twin beds. He started easy, just a lump under the sheets, then one arm out, with the nightgown strap falling down. But her face, her lotion smell—these he couldn't get. He could make the bed look full of somebody, but he couldn't make it be her.

They got the ice cream, and Father made him finish it, walking down the wide empty street. When Father unlocked the door to their motel room, there she was, stretched out on her back in her blue quilted robe. A streetlight shone on her, and in that light, her face was pale blue, marble-cold, and still. Father crouched beside her, held her wrist a second.

"Sleeping," he said. "Your mother can sleep like nobody's business. So, you want me to tell you a story now, maybe *Jack and the Beanstalk*, or something—"

"No thank you," said Gabe. "Is she dead?"

"Gabe, son, please," said Father, "Did I scare you? No, son. She's alive and well, just a terrific sleeper." Then he slapped his hand to his forehead. "My God, Gabe, we forgot all about your dog," he said. "She's been in the car all this time. I can't believe we forgot her. Get your pajamas on—I'll just run out there and take her for a little stroll, and put her back in the car. She'll be fine, Gabe. Fine."

"Is she really alive?" Gabe asked, but Father was already out the door.

GABE SAT UP IN THE DARK. Behind him, the Chief gazed down with unhappy eyes, his mouth pursed tight like he'd waited too long for something good to happen. There was a sudden low noise, a line of light under the bathroom door. Mother's bed was empty, the covers thrown back. In the other bed Father slept, his face toward the wall. Gabe walked over to the bathroom door.

"Mama," he said. "We saw a lady who looked like you—"

"Gabe, hush," she said, opening the door. "Is your father awake?"

"No," he said. "Are you having the baby now?"

"Not yet, no, sweetie. Don't wake him up, he needs his sleep for driving."

"Did he die?"

She looked at him sharply. "Did who die?"

"Harry Weiss, the Jewish Handcuff King. Did he die from the kick in his stomach?"

"Oh, Houdini," she said, giving him a hug. "The doctor said he should go straight to the hospital, but he refused. *The show must go on*, that's what he said to them."

"So he didn't die?"

"Well, he did, yes. But not right then. But listen, everything's fine. You'll like the baby, you'll like California. I promise."

"I guess so," he said. "But the lady looked just like you, and then—"

She smiled, and put her finger to her lips. "I'll tell you a secret. They say we all have a double somewhere, a person who looks just like us. Isn't that funny? Mine is right here in Nowhereville."

THE NEXT MORNING, before he opened his eyes, he felt it: a bright, ticking emptiness in the room, as if both Mother and Father had vanished, leaving him alone. But when he opened his eyes and looked around, everything was as before. He could hear Mother in the bathroom. Father was bent over one bed, filling a suitcase.

"Your little friend had a tough night," he whispered to Gabe. "She got sick, in the car. But I cleaned it all up and your mother will never know. Our secret, okay? She'd be upset."

She came out of the bathroom then. She smiled at Gabe and put her finger to her lips. He nodded, and looked from one to the other. He had a secret from each of them now.

As they got into the car, Father opened a new guidebook. "Today's the day," he said, and held it up high so Gabe could see the crumbling pink castle, and a big dull black bell. "There are churches like that, called missions, all over the state. I wish I could tell you what California did for me. I felt different there. It was like a refuge."

Mother looked at him, her eyes wide. "A refuge," she said. "Would you mind explaining that?"

Father started to say something, when Mother broke in again.

"Actually, don't tell me," she said. "Gabe, why don't you sit up front with your father, so you can see the ocean first. I'll take a nap in the back."

Father arranged it all: he put two pillows under Gabe, and patted his shoulder. "Here we go, son."

At first Gabe missed his kingdom, the dust angels and dark creases, the canyons and cliffs. But soon enough he was looking out the window as Father wanted him to. The pink earth was gone. Cracked dried mud appeared, dark green bushes, hills of yellow flowers.

"Now you can see! Why didn't I think of it earlier?" said Father. He turned the radio dial until it came to the beautiful rushing voice again. Trumpets, and a woman's voice crying out a song. "That's all I was trying to say," said Father. "Lots of feeling in their music. Maybe I'm a peasant, but is it so terrible that I like it?"

They rode along for a while, just listening. Father pointed out the big orange groves, and told Gabe to sniff the air. "Too bad your mother's not awake," he said. "Maybe the smell would cheer her up."

At sunset, Father said, very quietly this time, "Thar she blows," and pointed at a thin band of blue getting wider, until beside them that was all there was: a strip of pale sand, and water—so much water it looked like a lake with no end. Father pulled over and stopped the car, turned off the engine.

"Your first real beach. What do you think?"

When had Mother awakened? Because she was leaning forward now, leaning over the front seat, looking at the side of Father's face. She touched it once, lightly, as if there were a mark on him, a scar she'd never noticed before. "Spanish gold, Spanish music. That's a hint, isn't it? You met somebody. Just say yes or no, and I'll live with it."

Father shook his head. "There's nothing to tell. But what about you? What was all that about Houdini? Were you trying to tell me something?"

"With me it's a big fantastic nothing," she said. "Nothing but smoke and mirrors and everlasting innocence. But you. You've changed. I can tell. God, just a minute, I need some air."

She opened the car door.

"Clara, the dog—" cried Father, but it was too late. The dog gave a hoarse yelp, leaped out, and headed straight for the water.

"Daddy," cried Gabe. "Dad-dy!"

But Father was reaching into the backseat, trying to take Mother's hand. "Clara, Clara, listen to me. There's nobody else. I'm innocent, too. I swear."

She was sobbing. "You're not. It had to happen, I see that now."

That was when Gabe opened his door and slid out of the car. He was headed for the silvery dark blue, the lip of white foam curling and crashing on the sand, where the dog—his Longo—appeared and disappeared in the water.

Just as he hit the first small wave, hands gripped his middle, holding him tight. Father's voice, ragged and loud, reached around him like a rope.

"Let go," cried Gabe. Because the dog's head had popped up again next to him, and he could see her little mouth wide open, taking in water. Gabe slithered under and out of Father's grip, straight into the shock of white foamy cold, letting it rush at him, further and further up his chest, until a white wave came at him, and sucked him under. Then there was a weird quiet, and he felt himself lightly jostled, no longer cold.

For a moment no one could find him; he'd disappeared into a water tank like the one in Mother's story. It was peaceful there. He could just be. Then he felt the water dragging against him, rushing away, and he was high above it, hanging in the cold air.

"I've got you. Hold on."

It was Father again, his shirt plastered against his skin, and one arm tight across Gabe's stomach, pulling him, skimming him across the dark blue, the white foam swirling on it, breaking up in the dark.

Gabe was held above a big wave, Father's fingers digging into his ribs.

"My God, enough," cried Father, in a voice bigger than anything Gabe had heard before. "She's a water dog, she knows how to swim. That's why I got her! Look—she's headed our way!"

Father's strength was clear; he couldn't be fought. Gabe felt himself hauled and turned away from the dark blue, from the surprise of that quiet place under the waves. He could only see the beach, where Mother stood, one hand on the car door, and the other to her mouth, not a sound coming out. Gabe started to go limp in Father's arms when the dog turned away from them and began to paddle with all her might, straight out to sea.

"Daddy, put me down," cried Gabe, and gave one great last wriggle, the one that should have broken him free.

But Father had him firmly in both hands. He wasn't shouting anymore, but simply lifting Gabe higher and higher into the air. From one angle, it was clear that Father was saving him, holding him high above an oncoming wave. But from another, it must have looked like he was trying to hand his boy right up to God, and be done with him, with all of us, for good.

ANNUNCIATION

————

When I was thirteen, a girl visited my brother in secret. They'd met in Statistics that spring at Berkeley: she was Catholic, Asian, and, he said, prettier than our parents would like. On her side there were reasons too: she told Gabe her father would disown her if she dated a white guy, although Gabe's being Jewish might be the saving grace. Her father was a chef in San Francisco's Chinatown, and had recently remarked that Jews were his favorite customers: on Sunday nights they took the big tables, and always ordered more than they could eat. Over-ordering was a sign of family happiness, he'd said, giving her a look that could mean Jewish boys were exempt, or be an obscure double warning meant just for her. With her dad, she told Gabe, you could never really tell.

I was at the age where being disowned is nothing you wouldn't want. Privately, I imagined the risks Cheryl Owang might take: meeting my brother in the restaurant while her father gutted fish and chopped meat behind a swinging door. Her bare arms would be damp, smelling of ginger and raw chicken, and she'd kiss Gabe—only once—and push him out onto the sidewalk. "My father," she'd cry, leaving my brother with the smell on his own hands now, to drive him crazy until he saw her again.

At our house, there was no hope of being this sexy and exotic. After dinner, my father sat in his leather chair, making notes in the margins of his medical magazines. He napped all Saturday afternoon, waking up only to accuse me of taking the spring issue of *American Physician* or drinking the last of the juice. If I sat on the beach with a boy from my class, I'd see my father standing on our deck, his binoculars pointed our way. Afterward, he was waiting for me at the screen door, his hair crazy and windblown, his eye- brows raised as if I'd given him a mortal wound. "Watch your step," he'd say. "You don't know what you're getting into." Once he gripped my arm and said, "Slow it down, or you won't even get the chance at community college."

"I haven't done anything," I said, but my brother later said even this was too much. The best policy was not to reply. "If you answer them," he said, "things just get more complicated." So I practiced looking at my father the way Gabe did, a stoic, blank expression—the trick was not to blink, and never, never smile: this might be taken as surrender. If my mother were nearby, she'd beckon me into the next room. "Try not to aggravate him," she said. "He's going through a phase."

She frowned at me, and put her cool hand on my forehead as

if I were the one who needed my temperature taken. "How do you feel?" she asked, and I said okay, fine, though I wanted to tell her how for weeks my skin had been crawling with a dirty feeling that made me wish I could scrape it off and get a new one. At such moments we'd hear my father stirring on the couch. "What are you two talking about now?" he'd cry. "Why is everybody so goddamn secretive around here?" My mother shook her head. "Tell me what it is about life, Rachel," she said dreamily, stroking my hair. "Nothing for ages, then everything at once."

I was dying to confess something to her—anything—and nearly said that I couldn't wait for Cheryl Owang to get to us. But I held back, and later, in my own bed, allowed myself to think that at that very moment, a girl my own size was climbing out her bedroom window, dropping her small overnight case onto the lawn and taking in the sharp night air as she let herself down by knotted sheets. This was from a book I'd just read, which I could open at random to find the words *voluptuous, inflamed,* and *ravished.* I closed my eyes and went on: the girl, now wearing a dark jacket, would walk to the Greyhound station, and just as she boarded the bus, her father would be opening her bedroom door, shouting, "She's done it, the little slut's actually escaped."

"Slut, slut," I said into the darkness, surprised at the ordinary and brutal sound the word made coming out of my mouth.

I KNEW BETTER THAN TO BOTHER GABE with any of this. When I passed him in the hallway, he gazed angrily at me as if I had disturbed him during one of his problem sets. I guessed that this was what happened to a person whose life might be about to begin, who could pinpoint the day on which he would first unhook a girl's bra and help her step out of her panties. A tiny burning point grazed the center of my back when I imagined a boy doing this to me. I chose carefully—a tall, lanky boy from my class with whom I had never spoken, and could safely count on never knowing—and held my breath through the aching in my breasts and legs that was like the beginning of the flu.

This was nothing to my brother's suffering in the week before Cheryl's arrival. His hands shook and his eyes were wet and sad, like a skinny dog's. He changed his clothes several times a day, trying old ripped jeans and a flannel shirt, then the new khakis my mother had bought him, with a faded blue workshirt that I thought went with his eyes, though I did not tell him this. Between lunch and dinner (he was pale with hunger, then refused to eat) he roamed the house, opening closets and shutting them again, wedging himself between a door and a wall, then asking if I could see him. If I had behaved this way, he would have pummeled me.

It turned out he wasn't worried about Dad, who, he said, would probably sleep through the important parts of the weekend. It was our mother who made him nervous. Lately, her instinct for hidden plots had increased; she was forever appearing at Gabe's bedroom door when he least expected her, her mouth set in a small straight line as she stood there, her arms crossed as if to say, "Give it up, now; I know everything." She threw open his closet doors and dumped out the piles of clothes until she came to the dirty magazines. For these her eyes went bright and she said, "Just get rid of them. What I don't need is chaos." She searched his desk drawers when he wasn't there, and once came to my room to ask me if I'd noticed any odd behavior. "He's completely antisocial," she said. "It could be marijuana, or something else. I don't know why we let him go to Berkeley."

But the worst, Gabe told me, was that she was always sitting down on the extra twin bed in his room, smoothing down the bedspread and asking if he'd met anybody special yet. "You don't have to tell me right away," she said. "But I'd be happy to invite her down for a weekend."

This had cured him of any illusions, he said. It was obvious how things would go if he brought a girl home for a real visit, aboveboard. I could see it too: our mother would fix up the guest room as she did for out-of-state guests, with flowered sheets and glass bowls filled with kiwis and cherries; she'd arrange a whole morning of clothes shopping at the new Island Plaza, and finish the girl off with a seafood dinner out with all of us. After this, how would anybody have the nerve to go all the way with my brother, down in the gritty sand on an old towel, or maybe—to really risk it—on the extra twin in his own room, at night when the house was quiet.

Cheryl was to take the Greyhound to her cousins' in Santa Ana. Gabe would pick her up every day, and bring her back to them late at night. I was to be the lookout. I had hoped to hide her in my room overnight, but Gabe said with our mother the way she was just then, you couldn't take dumb chances. He shrugged: he had a way of defeating me just when I thought I'd taken his position.

——

WE WERE EARLY GETTING TO SANTA ANA even with Gabe driving forty miles an hour on the freeway, both hands gripping the wheel, not like any guy I'd ever heard of. "Keep an eye out for cops, Shrimp," he said, as if we were in some crime thriller, going ninety in a stolen car. As we drove inland, the houses got smaller and squarer, losing their gables and additions and sloping lawns until the 14000 block of Paso Robles Street. I hadn't known that street numbers could get so long. The sky was blank behind the small houses and the skinny bent palms, and I looked down, suddenly embarrassed by my matching seersucker shirt and shorts and the white wicker purse, what my mother called "a cute ensemble."

"I wore the wrong thing," I said. "You go ahead."

Gabe didn't answer right away. He was squinting at the houses and rubbing his palms across his jeans. His fingers on the dark cloth looked tender and unprotected.

"You're okay," he said. "Just try not to stare or say anything stupid." Then he sighed. "It's a different way of life, Rachel. A lot less crap."

Three cousins met us at the kitchen door, though later I thought of them as more than three—a whole clan of women, that's the way it felt. They were big, noisy girls who seemed to have been out in the world a long time already: they wore bright polyester slacks and flowered tops, and three or four rings on each hand.

"Neat outfit," the smallest cousin said to me at the door. "I saw that the other day, really cute."

For a minute we crowded there, unable to move, and I

smelled the rich, dense odors of whatever they were cooking: ginger, garlic, a sweet spice I didn't recognize. "Let them in, ladies," said a husky voice, and I looked up to see another girl putting her arm around my brother. She was the biggest of all of them, and wore a flowered sarong that made her look like a priestess, her arms and bare throat smooth, luxuriously fat.

"I'm Lourdes," she said in a voice I wanted to keep hearing. It was deep, and edged with a velvety burr. "Hang on, boy," she said. "We've sent the parents out for the day, and our little Honeycup's on the next bus in." She led us through the kitchen to a sitting room, and patted a long orange couch. "Sit," she said. "We're making something special." And she moved out of the room, the other girls following her like a bright flock.

"Honeycup?" I whispered to Gabe. "Do they mean Cheryl?"

"I guess," he said. "I've never heard that before." He wiped his hands on his jeans again and took a breath. "The family's Chinese Malaysian," he said in a ragged voice. "It's an island culture, totally different. The parents came over to escape persecution."

"Like our grandparents leaving Russia," I said.

He shot me a dark look. "No," he said. "Do me a favor and don't try to be friendly like Mom."

The cousins were filing back into the room, led by Lourdes, who handed my brother a bowl of soup. "Don't ask," she said, flicking her eyes up and down at him. "It makes boys grow up big and strong." Then she started to laugh, and held her wide dimpled hand to her mouth, full of a powerful, secret confidence. As she settled herself in a chair, she fluttered her eyelids dramatically, and I could see that at any moment now she might change her mind about us. But she was smiling at Gabe. "Not bad," she said. "Maybe a little underweight." She clapped her hands. "Eat, eat before she gets here and sees what a skinny dude you are."

Gabe sipped cautiously at the soup, and I could see his fingers trembling on the sides of the bowl. The cousins chattered shyly and giggled as we all ate—the sort of girl behavior that usually made my brother roll his eyes and feign sickness. But he seemed not to notice, and looked almost handsome, his eyes bright against his flushed skin. When he complimented Lourdes on the soup, he didn't look like my brother at all, but like a modest tourist who has learned the ceremonies of a country without fuss. He was happier than I'd ever seen him, and I saw that he was capable of getting married in a language he didn't understand with a garland of tropical flowers around his neck. He wouldn't miss us: he would sigh as he had outside the cousins' house, relieved of our family and the house on the beach cliff. It impressed me, and made me lonely in a new, somber way, to think how far he might go.

Cheryl arrived an hour later. She was smaller than her cousins, boyish in her jeans and a workshirt until she moved her hair out of her face and laughed at my brother in a mild, apologetic voice. That was when I saw how beautiful she was. There was a little silence, like a tribute, and she let her smooth hair fall over her face again. The cousins made more noise than ever, swarming around her, taking her duffel bag, pushing her toward the bathroom to "freshen up." Even the shy youngest one was familiar with my brother now, coming back to sit on the sofa, tapping him on the arm.

"Watch out for Lourdes if anything happens to Honeycup," she said, swinging her legs. "She's her guardian angel."

Then Cheryl came out of the bathroom wearing a short flowered cover-up and sandals, and they stopped joking. My brother cleared his throat and announced that we were taking Cheryl to the beach for the day. Lourdes came forward with three bottles of suntan lotion and a straw hat, kissing Cheryl as if she were going on a long journey. As we walked out the front door, Cheryl turned around. "Don't call me Honeycup in front of *them*," she whispered harshly. I turned to see if Gabe had heard it, too.

But he was looking at her with a flat, blinded look. "Let's go," he said, touching her bare shoulder. He hadn't heard anything.

THAT DAY MY BROTHER AND CHERYL had it exactly right, and must have known it, because they both seemed to be holding something off. We took Cheryl down to the north end of the state beach below our house, where all the families from inland towns set up their towels and umbrellas, and we wouldn't be watched by anyone we knew. I unfurled my towel at a short distance from my brother and Cheryl. I was not unhappy: I imagined my friends at the other end, laying out their towels in the old arrangements, waiting for a boy to walk up and invite one of them to the snack stand, or out to swim; how after one girl left, the rest of us would shake out our towels and spread them neatly again, filling in the gap. There was always a little stinging pain mixed in with the relief of not having been chosen yet, and I was glad to be out of it for a day, unobserved. I lay down on my belly and sifted the sand through my fingers, pretending deep

143

absorption and finally falling into the dreaminess of my own pretense, until Cheryl appeared above me, hugging her arms across her chest. She was wearing a bright flowered bikini, new and starchy stiff, and hunched her shoulders a little, as if she expected the straps to slip off at any minute.

"Lourdes bought me this—it's kind of too much, isn't it," she said.

"It's nice."

She ignored this. "Your big brother's afraid to go in the water," she whispered. "I think he's worried his trunks will look funny wet."

She pulled me up and we ran hard into the waves, pretending we didn't feel the cold shock, and I knew we were showing off for Gabe. I turned around and saw him standing beside his towel, skinny and pale in his swim trunks, his hands hanging awkwardly at his sides. Cheryl turned and saw him, too, then told me, in a rush, how they'd met, that my brother was the shyest cute guy she'd ever known: most cute guys knew what they had going, and this made them jerks. But my brother hadn't even tried to kiss her yet, she said, hugging her arms to her chest again.

"Has he had any girlfriends before me, do you know? I mean, is he—" She put her hand up to shade her eyes, then dropped it as if this gesture wasn't the one she wanted. "Never mind. I don't want to know. I just hope I don't get nailed by my dad."

She took a deep, shuddering breath as if preparing to submerge herself under the waves. There was hard light on her face, and for a moment, her expression was bitter and private, like my mother's when she didn't think anybody was looking. I saw that she wasn't afraid of her father or of anything: the more trouble and danger, the better. I wanted to run from her, back to my brother, speak to him before she did, though I couldn't think of what I would say. Then she snapped out of it, hopping on one foot in the water, trying to keep the waves from reaching her hips. "Aren't you freezing?" she said. "Let's go back."

Out of the water, she looked different again: smaller, delicate. She was exactly my height but had to weigh less, her arms were so thin, her wrists so tiny. I shivered, seeing now the little silver cross against her throat. It made her look more naked, and more foreign, too. As we walked up, Gabe was watching us with a stern expression, as if he'd made a decision while we were gone. Standing beside him, Cheryl curved her shoulders in, making herself even tinier, and when he teased her about her bright bikini, she put her fists up against his chest like a baby fake-fighting. Gabe was looking at her with a fierceness I'd never seen before, and at that moment, he bent unexpectedly to brush sand from the middle of her back. My body went suddenly rigid, electric. I knew I was seeing the beginning of things, and wasn't sorry when Gabe squinted at me. "Later, Shrimp," he said.

Once I got far enough away, I turned to look. They were already lying down on their sides, facing each other, but at that moment, as if by signal, Cheryl raised herself up by one hand and waved in my direction. Then she dropped down out of sight, and I couldn't find her again on the crowded beach.

FOR TWO DAYS, THEY DID NOTHING MORE than kiss, or brush their hands across each other's arms. Gabe still couldn't eat, and I

145

don't think he slept either. I heard him getting up in the night and turning over as if he could no longer get comfortable in his own bed. My mother pulled me aside in the hallway and put her hand on my shoulder—she knew I couldn't resist her then. "Tell your brother," she said, "that whatever it is, he shouldn't be afraid to tell me. Drugs, or God knows what, and we don't have to tell your father." Then she put her finger under my chin and looked me steadily in the eye. "Codes of honor aside," she said. "If he's in some trouble, we've got to know to help him."

I shrugged, and said in my most childish voice that he never told me anything but was still calling me Shrimp. Could she do anything about this? I was stunned by the ease of my subterfuge, and waited to be caught, but she only gave me a last, shrewd look and said she would speak to him if, in return, I would tell her if I heard or saw anything significant. "For everybody's sake," she said. "And I'm sure you know what I mean." I nodded, and imagined my parents lying in wait for me, gripping my arms and warning me how easy it was to get pregnant, and if this happened, they'd have no choice but to send me away, to have the baby in secret. I stood in the dark hallway long after she'd gone, imagining a passionate embrace with the boy from my class, his hands on my back, then almost immediately, resting tenderly on my slightly swollen belly. Beyond this I could not think. I was alone again in the ticking quiet of the hallway, feeling my scalp already creeping with dirt though I'd just washed my hair that morning.

GABE WANTED TO TAKE CHERYL OWANG down to the beach at midnight to hunt for grunion, the little silver fish that came in on the tide once or twice a summer. He'd been checking the newspaper for days, and had taken it as a sign when he saw the headline *The Grunion are Running!* that Saturday. The occasion was going to be my true test of usefulness. I was to come along, and keep an eye on our house from the beach: if I noticed signs of activity, I was to flick my flashlight beam twice, and precede the lovers up the beach stairs. Gabe would stay out on the deck, and I was to hide Cheryl in my room until further advised.

It is always a particular kind of night when the grunion run: a low tide, a moon lying close to the water, so you are deceived into thinking the little silver flashes are the fish themselves. The hunters stand in the wet sand, holding buckets and flashlights and staring down at their own feet. Every once in a while someone hisses, "Here they come!" but as the waves pull back, it's only the moonlight lapping silver on the small waves and rivulets of sand. Then suddenly, up and down the beach, people are whooping and giggling, and around your feet tiny slippery fish, the females, stand straight up in the sand, twisting back and forth, digging themselves in to bury their eggs, tickling your ankles delicately. You can never be fully prepared for this moment, for the life working under your feet, and that night, when I pulled my first one out of the sand, it left a shining streak of eggs across my palm. "No," I cried aloud, dropping the fish. It began wriggling again, digging itself into the sand, and I felt a little sick seeing the urgent, desperate curving of its body.

Cheryl stood nearby, wearing my brother's windbreaker, while he rushed the low water expertly with his bucket. Once she bent for a grunion, but it slipped from her grasp almost immediately. It seemed to me that she opened her hand the moment it touched the fish, taking it and letting it go all in one motion. She looked thin-armed, angular in the moonlight, her hair falling across her face as it had that first day, only this time it made her seem awkward and childish. Gabe set his bucket down and grabbed her arms, pinning them behind her back. "Ss-stop it," she whispered, gliding backward on the sand like a skater. "Stop what?" Gabe cried, and she bucked against him, kicking his shins. The water looked like a fake backdrop, their figures against it lit by the hunters' separate flashing lights. Then she said something I couldn't hear, and broke free, and my brother was running after her down the beach.

For a long time I sat at the foot of the beach stairs with the bucket, my brother's fish flipping hopelessly in the water—we were saving them as evidence if our mother had questions. Gabe and Cheryl eventually came back down the beach with their arms around each other, walking up into the dry sand, away from the hunters and their lights. They stopped just far enough away that I saw their figures as they sat, then lay down, in the sand. But between the low hissing of the waves I thought I heard the rustling of Cheryl's windbreaker, and then, a little later, a single, odd cry. I felt the slight sickness of the grunion-hunting come back, though what was wrong about it all I could not say, only that I saw Cheryl bent over the sand as she let go of the squirming fish, and felt its wild movement thrumming in my own abdomen, a lonely secret discomfort that might belong to Cheryl, too, though she'd never confess to anyone.

I got up then, and went down among the groups of grunion

hunters with their flashlights waving in crazy, Morse code games. They called to each other, their voices easy, celebratory, as if they were glad the grunion were gone, that the tide had closed over something more shocking than anybody had bargained for. I was standing among them, looking back at our house, trying to see it as the house of strangers, everyone asleep now as they should be, asleep and comfortable, when I realized that the kitchen light was on, then the one in Gabe's room, then mine. I started running, flashing my little light as I went, already knowing it to be my father's discovery. When I got to them, they were already sitting up, and Cheryl was trembling, her arm caught in the sleeve of Gabe's jacket. "I swear to God," she cried. "It's like he knows everything." We were running up the stairs when I realized she was talking about her own father, and not mine.

It turned out that my father had been awake, sitting at the kitchen table in the dark when he heard a tapping on my brother's bedroom window. When we got to the deck, we saw Lourdes inside our living room, wearing a hooded sweatshirt and standing between our parents, her face impassive except for one moment when she glanced around our living room and frowned at the furniture. As we came in, she gave me that same disapproving frown.

"No joke," she said. "You kids live here?" Gabe was standing a few feet back with Cheryl, who was squirming as if he had her arms pinned again. Gabe shrugged, looking at the carpet between Lourdes and himself.

"It's no big deal," he said.

"Right," said Lourdes, with a short laugh.

My father moved away from us, his hair ruffled like an old bird's, his eyebrows gathered. He stood with his legs apart, but they were skinny and pale below his bathrobe, and the sash tied so loosely that it might at any moment come apart. I wanted to close my eyes and open them again to see him fully dressed as if for work, his hair neatly combed and his face stern and knowing, ready to give us all a lecture. Gabe seemed to be waiting for this, too, his hands on Cheryl's shoulders now, as if he'd remembered the way movie heroes stood when they were protecting their sweethearts from intruders.

"Dad, Mom," he said. "This is a friend of mine, Cheryl Owang. She's a chem major—"

"Don't bother," my father said, but there was no force in his voice, nothing to dread. He seemed out of breath just from this, and turned away from us toward his and my mother's bedroom.

"Honey," said my mother. "Come back. There's no need—"

But he was already gone, moving away as if we were no part of his life.

My brother let go of Cheryl then, and my mother came across to hug her. Lourdes gazed at the two of them, her face still and careful, revealing nothing.

"Well, Honeycup, your daddy called," she said. "I told him you were asleep, but I don't think he bought it." Then she looked around again, at our draperies and carpeting, at the black-lacquered vase beside the tiled hearth, and at my brother, who wasn't looking at anyone. She reached forward and pulled Cheryl away from our mother with three rough little tugs. "Come on, girl," she said. "Your little adventure with the rich white folks is over."

"This is my house," said my mother. "Let's just wait a minute."

I thought she would make a speech, but she just asked who would like a cup of hot chocolate. She waited with such dignity that no one could refuse her. She heated it up, and we sat at the table drinking from the china cups that had, before this moment, been precious to me because of the exotic Japanese willow painted on one side. Nobody spoke. I felt foolish handling the tiny perfect cup, waiting for my mother to release us. At last, Lourdes stood up and looked at Cheryl, and in a second my mother was at Cheryl's side, inviting her to spend the night. Lourdes shrugged, murmured something to Cheryl, and a moment later, was gone. My mother turned to Gabe. Her face was shuttered, expressionless, just as Cheryl's had been in the water, making you wonder what she knew. She said nothing, just looked at him until he skulked away toward his room.

We helped her wash the cups, and then she brought out her favorite flowered sheets, making up the extra bed in my room. Gabe was in his, I knew, but utterly silent. Later, he would show up and kneel at Cheryl's bedside, and she would pretend to be asleep until he gave up and went away. But for the moment it was my mother and Cheryl and me, my mother smoothing down the sheets as if for one of my own friends, a first spending of the night, and before she left, she kissed each of us on the cheek. Cheryl shook her head, her face streaky with tears. "Oh," she said. "I like it here. I wish I could stay awhile."

Lourdes came back for Cheryl just before daybreak. She came to my window, the gray hood of her sweatshirt framing her face as it must have the night before, like that of a messenger in an old drama, coming to warn the lovers that the authorities were on their trail. "Hurry," she whispered, and gestured up the hill, above the beach cliff, where she'd parked her car.

As she climbed out my bedroom window out onto the deck, Cheryl was trembling. She kissed me lightly on the forehead and said, "Tell your cute brother I'm not that mad at him. And anyway, it's not like I was going to be the great love of his life." She smiled, but her face was damp with tears. "You're my little sister," she said, and I nearly fainted with pleasure. I loved her, I thought, more than Gabe ever could. Closing my window, I wished myself in her place, going north on that bus, leaning my cheek against the cool window while other passengers, men and women with unknowable lives, slept or told each other stories, making them better or more horrible than real life, feeling a funny shiver listening to those voices that were sometimes calm, sometimes excited. I imagined a strange man, no boy I knew, in the seat next to mine, moving his hand over slyly to touch my knee. My hands tingled, and I shook my head. I'm not ready, okay? I whispered, alone in my bed. Not yet. I lay back and pulled the covers up tight, touching the high-buttoned collar of my nightgown and the cuffs long and ruffled, hiding my wrists. I wondered if Cheryl were feeling anything like this, leaning back with her eyes closed on that bus, moving on to whatever was going to happen to her next.

GOD'S SPIES

E very morning that summer my father got up in the dark, made himself a cup of instant, and took it out on the deck of the beach house, to listen to the waves rushing up and back. He called this "communing with the sea," and it was true that as he stood there, his face went blank, as if he were picking up a private signal—like that high ringing in the ears that used to close me up like a shell when I was younger, just for a few seconds. "A little fluid in the ear," he told me once, frowning. "Remind me to check it out, just routine." But I didn't want him to. It was a high, strange song I loved, and even he, a medical man, had an unscientific name for it: "God's dial tone." I still think of him whenever I hear it. It never lasts, though I try to hang on to it, the way I did that summer, when I was fifteen and had the feeling I was finally getting to know him.

One of those mornings, woken by no alarm, I remember the sky and water having this pale, abandoned look—*bereft of the night*, I thought to myself, and was briefly pleased. My father was moving around upstairs, opening the sliding door to the deck. I went upstairs and we stood together, leaning on the rails. This felt like a test: could I stand there as long as he did without saying something? Not until the light spread all the way across the water did he turn to me. "What are you doing up at this hour? Go back to bed—your mother's still out cold." And he went back inside, turned on the television for the financial news, and called his broker back east.

That day, his strength lasted straight through breakfast; he didn't start to fade until eight o'clock or so. "I'll just rest a minute," he said. "Then I'll be ready to hit the trail." As we ate, he scanned our faces the way he scanned the newspapers for a new stock venture. It was only my mother and me, and also Grandma Eva, who was visiting that summer from Indiana. Gabe was off at summer biology camp, with his jars of seawater, his special notebooks. He'd come home for a weekend once, but even then, we hardly saw him. He'd show up for meals, bearing on his swim trunks traces of seaweed, and on his ankles, glistening bracelets of sand. He carried a clipboard under his arms at all times, plus one of the jars of seawater for unexpected specimens. What else was left to do with the ocean? I consoled myself that he might be the expert on the Pacific, but someday I would have the whole story of our family, with all its secrets. Gabe could go ahead and beg me—I would give him nothing.

In the kitchen, my mother moved dreamily, bringing things

to the table, then frowning at them as if to keep them from floating off. She was still in thrall to the night, her throat pale and
freckled above her bathrobe, an exhausted diva with her hair
turbaned up, her powers pale and useless in daylight. My father's
gaze fell on her and he said lazily, "I almost forgot to tell you. I
took a little chance and signed you up for the Pageant."

My mother looked at him, and waited.

"An Evening with the Masters," he said. Then he turned to
me. "Look at her. She could've been a model for any one of those
guys—Renoir, or Whosits."

She blinked at him as if she might be about to wake up, but
Eva was tapping her spoon lightly on the table. "I'd let him have
his way on this one," she said. She looked intently at my mother,
as if she could hypnotize her into behaving like a normal wife.

My mother sighed. "What do they make you do?"

OF COURSE SHE KNEW. It was a thing we loved, my father and me
especially. In the next town down-coast, during the Summer Art
Festival, regular citizens like ourselves were outfitted with
costumes and made up to look like the figures in famous paintings and sculptures. I loved the spectacle of those nights: the
blue of the sky at dusk, the hush in the amphitheater as the klieg
lights went down, and a deep, mellifluous voice flooded the steep
shell, startling everyone. "The rabbi should sound that good," my
father used to say. He took me once to a dress rehearsal, and we
found the announcer's booth backstage. I had never seen my father
so excited. What manner of man would have such a voice, he
wanted to know. But when the announcer turned around, he

was potbellied, with a florid face and a veiny, bulbous nose. Even the booth he spoke from was a terrible disappointment to my father: it had pegboard walls, and little inspirational sayings tacked up everywhere. "Excuse me, my friends, I must away," the man said to us in his stage voice, but it sounded absurd and fake in the cramped room. He must have felt this, too, because he waved us away and lifted his headphones up, putting on an alert, fiercely inward face. "Ready when you are," he said, to some authority we couldn't see.

At that same rehearsal I saw a boy not much younger than myself riding a horse in a circus painting. He refused to come down out of his pose when the set was wheeled offstage. A stagehand poked his leg with a riding whip. "Hey, Champ," he shouted. "Wake up. It's over." On that boy's face as he let himself be handed down was a stony, beautiful expression. He had been somewhere else, and did not want to come back. He looked strange coming out of the painting, as if he'd been drugged and transported to another time, the one where he really belonged; he looked the way I felt when I was woken up out of dreams too soon. He was stubbornly blank, spoke to no one, could not be coddled or cajoled. Someday, I promised myself, that's how I'll be.

THE AFTERNOON OF THE AUDITION, my father couldn't come along. "I've got an appointment with some quack," he said. "No cause for alarm." My mother looked at him in surprise but he only smiled and leaned down to me. "I think your mother's nervous," he said. "Can you go with her for me? Be one of God's spies. That's nice—I like that. Where did I get that?"

"Shakespeare," I said severely, confidently, though in fact this was a wild guess.

He put his hand on my head. "Everything you know, your mother taught you," he said, his voice rough, burred. "You know that, don't you?"

"I don't know anything. Nobody ever tells me what's going on," I said, bitterly and not without calculation, hoping he'd tell me something he'd never told my mother, my brother, or anyone. But he only shrugged in his offhand way. He could do this: go from corny, gangster-movie intimacy—as if he were asking your help in some shady business deal—to a breathtaking distance, like he was an old mountain, and you, a speck in the valley far below.

He and Grandma Eva walked with us out to the car that afternoon. The pink audition notice fluttered out of my mother's purse, and he stuffed it back in for her.

"Don't be shy," he said. "Let them get a good look at you."

"Abe, it's not Broadway."

"Don't carp," said Eva, giving my mother a little shove. "Just go."

My father stood back from the car and gave a little parade wave as we backed down the driveway. My mother said in a quiet voice, "I wish he wouldn't do this. He's doomed to disappointment."

FROM OUR TOWN TO THEIRS, the world changed entirely. We had the flat sandy beach, and one long curved cliff above it. They had the rocky shoreline, the waves always crashing, the tree branches bent low and hard by winds we didn't get. The road south wound diabolically around the beach cliffs. My mother let everyone pass her, braking after each curve precisely as my father had taught her to. Moisture collected delicately above her mouth. She was the only redhead in our family, and my father had a kind of awe about her looks which she scorned. "Don't flatter me," she'd cry, as if he'd inadvertently wounded her. Maybe he thought the experience of modeling in the Pageant would give her some confidence. I imagined how the directors would take one look at her, and see exactly what my father did: that she was a beauty out of some lost era, straight out of Renoir's *Dance at Bougival*, a poster he had in his office at home. That would be my mother, with her milky complexion, her eyelids cast down in a maidenly way as she is tilted slightly back by her handsome partner, her dress in a graceful twist under the trees. A natural beauty, they'd say to her, where have you been hiding yourself? She'd have to smile at last, though her hands would rise in faint protest. "It was my husband's idea," she'd say. "When he gets an idea, nobody can stop him."

The road to the Festival Grove was overhung with a canopy of live oak and eucalyptus. Here the hills began, and glades of tall trees made a hushing sound to lull you, their long leaves thin as fingers pointing down. The Grove itself was a mile inland, far enough from the beach that you couldn't hear the rough banging of the waves.

As we got out of the car, my mother straightened her skirt and took a deep breath. "It's good to get away from all that chaos," she said.

"What chaos?" I said.

She looked at me in her new sleepy way. "What did I say? I meant the usual, Sweetie. I don't know what I meant."

For all her confusion she seemed to know exactly where to go, and threaded her way easily among the fiberboard booths of painters and sculptors under the eucalyptus trees. She barely glanced around her, but walked straight toward an enormous barnlike building. "Into the breach," she said, opening the door wide.

In the barn the crowd was enormous: not only grown-ups, but children too, and girls and boys my age with long tanned arms and drifty blond hair. There was something foreign about it, as if we'd fallen into a different country, whose people had long ago been initiated into an important secret. Nobody seemed to notice us, and my mother smiled as if this pleased her somehow. She got a cup of coffee and a paper name tag, and sat down in a metal chair against a wall, patting the seat beside her. On the walls behind us were pictures of the famous tableaux of previous Pageants, and my hopes rose as I imagined her cast in the part of a royal lady, perfectly erect in jewels and velvet, surrounded by maids and children. I was still picturing this when a man strolled over and looked her up and down.

"Clara Gershon," he said, ticking a line off his clipboard. "Do you have a problem with apparent nudity?"

My mother's hand came down on my shoulder so suddenly I flinched. She stood up. "This is my daughter Rachel."

"Ah, Persephone herself," he said, smiling at me as if we'd known each other for ages. He squatted beside my chair. "Listen, honey, Mom's going to be Ceres, the Goddess of the Corn, painted gold from head to toe. Flat-out spectacular. How are you with secrets?" He looked severely at me, but didn't wait for an answer. "Anonymity is crucial," he said, looking up at my mother. "The illusion must be complete. We have never yet had a failure."

He took her arm. "Come meet your Neptune."

"Rachel," said my mother. "Don't move. Stay right here. I'll be right back."

When she came back, she was even paler than usual. In her hand was a glossy color photograph of a man and woman, golden and naked, lounging on a giant jeweled crown.

"The world's gone crazy," she said. "Your father included. I swear I will never again put you in this position, but right now it's important to your father that I go through with this. I can't explain it right now, but can you promise me not to say a word at home?" She waved the photograph in the air. "I don't think he knows the particulars."

She had never before spoken to me this way: weighty, conspiratorial, trusting. I nodded, afraid to say anything and break the spell. With any luck, my mother would be a stark-naked, pure-gold earth goddess on a three-hundred-year-old saltcellar, the famous one of the Pageant, the pièce de résistance, according to the caption on the photograph. Golden Ceres she'd be, and facing at a distance of two feet, maximum, handsome and athletic Neptune, who leaned casually back with his trident held stiffly out. I noticed that Ceres didn't look as good as Neptune. Her breasts sagged, her back slumped a bit, she looked sad. I pointed this out to my mother, and she explained hastily how Ceres had lost her daughter to the God of the Underworld, and by some deal they made, got her back each spring for a while. She had every right to look that way.

"Like a kid in a divorce?" I said.

She looked at me wearily. "No," she said. "Like a kid in a myth. Look, you wanted to see Neptune, there he goes." She pointed out a broad-shouldered man in Bermuda shorts and sandals. She leaned down again. "He thinks he's God's gift," she said. "It doesn't seem to take much around here."

On the way home she told me how it had gone, how she'd wanted to sit down a moment, but there was nowhere at all. People swarmed, gathered. Neptune had leaned toward her. "It's hotter than Hades in here," he'd said, and waited for her to smile. She wasn't in the mood, and simply said, "Nice to meet you." But as she fled, an elegant woman her own age put a hand on her arm. She informed my mother that she herself was in a state of shock, having just found out she was going to be a Spanish royal personage having her hair done, smack in the middle of some prince's family—the painting was by Goya, or Velázquez, the name just now escaped her. Then she leaned closer. "I heard about you, poor dear," she said. "But don't worry. I hear they let you wear a little diaper. You won't actually be, you know, *naked*."

Secrecy, it turned out, did not sit well with my father. He was all right for the first couple of days, thought it was cute of us. Then, one afternoon, resting in his big leather chair, he called out suddenly to my mother, "Show me the fine print. Show me where it says, *And thy spouse shall remain in utter darkness until the big night.*

"Shall I have the director call you?" she said.

"He'll think I'm jealous."

My mother smiled. "Whose idea was this?"

"I didn't know how far they'd take it," he said. "You look like the cat that ate the canary."

For the next two weeks, everything went wrong for him. Promising deals soured, shares fell, a rock 'n' roll band he'd invested in was hauled in during a drug raid. He was having trouble at the office with a tricky diagnosis, and with my mother distracted, Grandma Eva took over the household. She closed all the blinds and curtains, and prepared heavy, old-fashioned meals: chicken and dumplings, noodle kugel, peas cooked until they were pale. "You need to be fortified," she said. "Your mother has no comprehension, never has."

One afternoon she called me into her bedroom. Before she'd come to stay with us, this had been an ordinary guest room, a place we threw our extra stuff when nobody was visiting. It had white walls and venetian blinds, and three small seascapes my father had bought at the Festival over the years. But Grandma kept the blinds drawn, and now the room had the muffled, sinister dark of a carnival booth, the television flickering a malevolent blue in the corner.

"Be good to your father," she said. "He's not feeling well, and could use a little attention."

"I knew it. Is it V.D., is that why nobody will say?"

"For God's sake, what do they teach you at school? Listen, they don't know exactly, but it's one of those things that usually strikes children." She looked at me grimly. "Leave it to your father to break the mold."

She was quiet a moment, then raised her hand in a royal gesture of dismissal. I stumbled out as if from a cave into blinding sunlight, and moved through the hall to the stairs. Above, I heard his voice. He was on the phone—with his broker, I figured, then remembered it would already be night in New York. I listened for familiar words, but heard none, and no gusto in his voice. He hung up then, and I heard him open the sliding door to the deck. Though he usually gave it a forceful shove, this time it made a forlorn swoosh, a sound like a car passing on a rainy street. By the time I came upstairs he was outside, no coffee cup in his hands. The television was still on, its jaunty music playing for no one, the numbers speeding past. I went out and stood beside him.

"Heavy trading on the market?" I said.

He sighed. "Don't bother your head with that garbage," he replied. "I don't know why I got into it. Listen, tell me about your mother. What painting is she in? I promise not to let on that I know."

"I'm under oath," I said. "From the director."

"For Crissakes," he shouted. "Why is she like this? And you! You were supposed to be my eyes and ears. What did I say?"

"You're the same way," I said. I held my breath; never before had I said such a thing to my father.

But he turned casually, as if he hadn't heard me. "I just had a brainstorm," he said. "Since you're so good at keeping secrets, here's one more."

I trembled. Now he would tell me, in his own words, what was wrong with him.

"A secret of our own. She can be in the dark herself, for a change."

"I'm ready, Dad," I said.

"Rachel, this is going to be spectacular. Just bear with me a day or so."

THE NEXT AFTERNOON, while she was in rehearsal, my father said that his plans had worked out, and I just needed to come with him down to the Festival Grove. I balked: what if she got let out of the barn for a coffee break, and ran into us? She'd think we were spying on her, and that I couldn't be trusted. My father smiled. "You've got what we call an overactive imagination," he said. "Take it from me, you're doing nothing wrong. In fact, you're giving her a little present. And it's got nothing whatever to do with her show, I give you my word of honor." He wanted Grandma Eva to come along, too, as "moral support," he said, and she agreed. On the drive down he pulled over at Inspiration Point, which looked out over a series of craggy tide pools. "Eva," he cried. "Get a load of this drop-off!" he said. But as the three of us stood there, he was the one who clung to the railing, and whose hair stuck out like a seagull's ruffled feathers. His trousers flapped wildly and I saw that he was pale, too quiet. He squinted at the roadside marker, and gazed down at the rocky tide pools until Grandma put her hand on his arm.

"Okay, on we go," he said, looking at me, his eyes strangely bright. "We're doing this for posterity."

AT THE FESTIVAL GROVE, we wandered among the booths of portraitists and potters until he found the one he was looking for: a short, stocky man with curly hair and intense black eyes.

"My God, it's Rasputin," Grandma whispered. "What does your father want with him?"

He smiled as if he'd heard her, and didn't mind the comparison in the least. All his paintings, I noticed, were of stormy ocean scenes. Even the brightest one, *Sunset at Santa Dominga*, was slate and blood-red. If you looked close, you could see a little dinghy broken up in the tide pools.

"Let's see what we've got here," he said, taking my arm.

He lifted my chin lightly upward, turned my face this way and that. "A nice exotic confusion," he said, his fingers warm on my skin. Then, as if I'd passed some test, he released me, and pointed to a short stool. When I was seated, he lifted my chin once more, turned my shoulders, and looked into my eyes. "Just like that," he said. "Hold still, and don't talk. Can you do that?" He put his hands on my shoulders once more—had I already moved? Grandma Eva flinched.

"Is it necessary to touch the child so often?"

The artist looked at me inquiringly.

I gave the merest shrug, so as not to ruin my pose, and he smiled. "Good. Very good."

My father pulled up two folding chairs and invited Eva to sit down with him. "Eva, Rachel, this is Paul Godinski," he said. "So, am I right, you'll do the portrait today, and put in the background later, so it looks like she's sitting on the tide pool rocks—you know that one called Sphinx Rock?"

Godinski nodded. "I know it well."

My father turned to me. "If it goes well, maybe we can take a break later and see what your mother's up to in the big rehearsal."

"It's against the rules," I said.

Godinski smiled a small, bitter smile. His eyes gleamed at me. "Rules are for breaking," he said.

The intensity of his gaze worked like a spell on me. The eucalyptus glade appeared slightly inflamed, a violence of blue and gold, and the voices of tourists and booth-artists seemed muted, miles away. The seagulls appeared to be flung around by an unseen hand. I felt achy, almost feverish, and wanted nothing more than to look at Godinski, at his deft, fast-moving hands particularly, but I knew he would never forgive me if I shifted. Grandma Eva, despite her best efforts, had fallen asleep, her arms draped on the sides of her folding chair. Her feet, in their open-toed, old-lady sandals, looked forlorn and unprotected among the acorns and old leaves.

"You need a break," Godinski said to me. "Go get a Coke or something," and at this Eva startled awake. My father was still asleep in his own chair, his head fallen to one side, his mouth open.

"I'll come with you," Eva said. "Is he safe there?"

Godinski cocked his head. "Safe from what?" he said.

Eva sighed. "Never mind. I asked the wrong person. Come, Rachel."

We were almost out of the Grove—nearly to the barn itself, when she turned to me. "This so-called Godinski is a menace," she said. "With a mind like that, what will he do with a human subject, a young girl, no less?"

I wanted to speak in his defense, so we could go back again, but I found I couldn't answer. He had forbidden me to speak, and I liked the way the world looked under my own silence.

"Why don't you show me the rehearsal hall," Eva said

casually. "I don't want to see your mother. I'm just thinking we'll know if your father wakes up and tries to sneak in."

She was almost inside the door; it was too late to stop her, and I couldn't muster the feeling of betrayal I knew I should have. It seemed correct—even safer, somehow—that Grandma Eva be in on the Pageant conspiracy.

The floors creaked as we approached a dim corner of the stage, from which we could hear voices, laughter. At first I wasn't sure what I was seeing. It looked like a parade float made of gold foil and with great red and blue glass pieces embedded in its sides—to look like jewels from a distance, I guessed. Two women were assisting a third, very carefully, as she stepped up over the side of it. They all laughed again. "I'm dripping," she said. This was my mother, my mother's voice. She was entirely naked, entirely gold. Another woman came up with a little brush and dapped more paint on her hands. "The Midas touch," said a man's voice, and he was naked, too.

"God in heaven," said Eva.

"The family isn't supposed to know," I said.

"You can say that again."

"You won't tell anyone."

"Indeed not," said Eva. "Wild horses, as they say."

"If we have to, we'll tell Dad she's in the Spanish painting. *The Family of the Infante Don Luis*—he'll like that."

"Naked on a saltcellar," said Eva.

"She's the Goddess of the Corn," I said.

She looked at me sharply. "Naked is naked. The day you forget is the day I drop dead."

When we got back to the booth, my father was still asleep. Godinski was in fact kneeling before him, and looked at us in amazement. "This guy can sleep like nobody. Is he all right?"

"No, actually, he isn't," said Eva. "You'd better help me wake him up."

I thought we'd have trouble tearing him away from the Festival Grove, that he'd wake up in a delirium and beg us take him to the rehearsal barn. But his forehead shone with sweat, and his hands were icy cold.

"I guess that's enough for one day," he said. "When did it get so hot?"

ALL THAT WEEK, I SAT FOR THE PORTRAIT, and every night as I lay in bed unable to sleep, the artist Godinski came to me with his fierce black eyes, his hot sandpaper fingers on my arm. They burned there, and I shivered all over. One night I awoke abruptly, not knowing I'd slept. I was no longer in my room, but standing outside my parents' bedroom door, which was slightly ajar. This was an old habit I thought I'd long since outgrown. There, as ever, were my parents' twin beds, my father in his, my mother standing over him in her bathrobe. But he didn't look like my father: he could have been a little boy sick in bed. I knew this from the sad, solicitous curve of her shoulders as she bent to him. I couldn't see my father's face, either, but his back moved a little, heaved, and her hand on his shoulder didn't move at all.

I don't remember saying anything, but she turned, no surprise in her face. "Rachel, do me a favor and go back to bed. It's three in the morning."

"Is Dad all right?" I asked.

"Just a little nausea," she said. "Something's going around—"

"A case of nerves," my father called out weakly. "I've got stage fright on your mother's behalf. Go! I expect to see you at the crack of dawn."

When I awoke at dawn and came upstairs, it was my mother who was pacing the living room, a cup of tea in her hand. I must have frightened her, coming up the stairs, because she gave me a wild look. "What woke you?" she said. "Why is it that all other teenagers in the world sleep late? Could you do that for me sometime?" Then she sighed. "Listen, tell Grandma when she wakes up—I'm taking your father to the doctor."

"What's he got," I asked.

She put her hand on my arm the way she'd done in the rehearsal barn. "They honest-to-God don't know, Rachel."

"Grandma says it's something children get."

She didn't say anything, just looked over my head a long minute. "Your grandmother isn't an expert in the field. I promise to tell you when we know." And she turned away fast.

MY PARENTS WERE HOME AGAIN BY AFTERNOON. Could my father have planned even this? Because just a few minutes before their car pulled up, Godinski appeared on our doorstep, a great square shape in brown paper leaning against his leg. He was asking Grandma Eva if he could come in, and to my astonishment, she refused. She simply folded her arms across her chest and said, with absolute seriousness, "Please come back later, when the master of the house is at home." But by then their car had pulled up, and my father was getting slowly out of the car, leaning on my mother's arm. He came to the front door like a king, and with great ceremony opened our front door for Godinski. "Welcome to my humble abode," he said, trying to smile, and my mother looked at all of us. "What's going on this time?" she said hoarsely, but my father was already headed for his big leather chair. "Go ahead and do the honors," he said to Godinski. "I forgot to say, it's a surprise for my wife."

Godinski slit the paper with a lazy flourish. It wasn't my mother who gasped, but Grandma Eva.

"I should have stopped him," she said to my mother. "But you married him. You know how he is."

I didn't see the problem. I liked the way I looked. I liked the almond shape he'd given my eyes, and the faint lavender shadows beneath, as if I'd been awake all night, thinking. It was who I wished I was, right down to the sea thrashing around me as I sat on Sphinx Rock, surrounded by nature's violence. I flushed with pleasure, and could not look at Godinski, lest he catch me in my vanity, and laugh out of his terrible depths of knowledge.

"Do you like it?" I asked my mother.

She smiled briefly. "It's quite dramatic," she said, taking my arm and nodding at Godinski at the same time. She drew me close as if I were a small child in need of protection. "You did a wonderful job. Has he paid you yet? We just got back from the hospital, or I'd invite you to stay—"

"Nonsense," said my father. "Stick around. I'll make you a drink."

Godinski shifted awkwardly from one foot to the other,

keeping his eyes down. My mother was looking at him intently. At last he spoke, in a rough, unused voice, and I realized he had not spoken to anyone else for hours, possibly the whole day. "Actually, I have to get back. I've got somebody coming at three—"

I followed him to the front door, and just as he opened it, I cleared my throat.

"So," I said, looking at him as steadily as I could. "Do I really look like that?"

"You will," he said. "Sooner than you think." And he looked me over once more, until my face went hot and I had to look away.

MY MOTHER ASKED MY FATHER not to hang the picture in our living room or even the hallway. "Look at the jagged rocks, look at her eyes! It's completely morbid, and doesn't look anything like her."

Grandma Eva stood up from the couch. "Not to mention it's bad luck to have a picture of the living in your house. I thought you knew that, Abe."

This seemed to give my father pause. "Fine," he said. "You leave me no choice. We'll put it in the guest room."

"The guest room," said Eva.

"There's a big open spot on the wall behind the bed," he said. "It's the perfect spot."

"Abe—" began my mother.

"Whose house is this?" he said. "Couldn't one thing be the way I'd like it?"

Eva blushed and looked at me. "Come downstairs with me," she said. "Now."

All that day and next, my father sulked. We all tiptoed

around him, waiting for a thaw, but he held himself aloof, and one afternoon, when Eva and my mother were out shopping, he hung the portrait where he'd said he would, right over my grandmother's bed. When she got back and saw it, she turned pale, but said nothing to him. To my mother she said, just once, "I wash my hands."

Not until the night of the Pageant did my father consent to speak to us. He had a slight headache, he said, but he wouldn't miss the show for anything. My mother, who had missed a rehearsal or two taking him to the doctor, begged him to "call a halt to the whole business," as she put it. "They have understudies," she said. "No harm done."

"Over my dead body."

"Abe," she cried, but she was looking at me.

"Weren't you supposed to be down there fifteen minutes ago?" he asked. "To get dressed and all?"

I looked at her then, but she wouldn't meet my eye.

Before she left, my mother laid out our clothes—my father's and mine—as she'd done when I was small, for grand occasions. "I'm not taking any chances with either of you," she said, waving goodbye as if she were going on a long trip. At six-thirty I knocked on the guest-room door, and as Eva opened it, the hall light flooded in, lighting up her bed and a corner of the portrait. Had she been sitting in the dark so she wouldn't have to see it? She had circles under her eyes and a pale, surprised face, as if she'd already suffered a year of sleeplessness under my sad gaze. She straightened my barrettes, and licked a finger to flatten my bangs. "Listen to me," she said. "You're not the tragic creature he made you out to be. Your eyes aren't like that at all. What is it with painters? They have no respect for reality."

My father was waiting for us beside the car, jingling his keys in his pocket. His hair was still damp and raked carefully across his bald spot. "Well, well," he said, helping Eva into the front seat. "The big night is here, the mystery about to be revealed."

"Don't count your chickens," she said, but he was already smiling a little, as if she'd announced some happy prophecy.

THE FESTIVAL AMPHITHEATER was lit golden-pink, like the inside of a conch shell. Streaky clouds moved across the sky, and the moon was just up, only a sliver.

Eva watched the stage closely. She rolled her program into a little tube and tapped it lightly against the armrest. "What's the point of such a program," she said in a loud and ragged voice. "She could be in anything, and we'll never know unless she deigns to tell us. I didn't raise her to be a sneaky person."

I looked down at my program. There was a list of partici-pants, in which I found my mother's name, and on the next page, a list of paintings and artists' names. What amazed me was that they could sustain the mystery: up until now I hadn't known how good adults could be at keeping secrets. I was beginning to see that they were better at keeping them than at letting them go.

The lights went down, the audience began to murmur, and the orchestra struck up something grand and classical. My father put his arm around my shoulder. "Your mother would know what this is," he said proudly. "She always knows."

Out of darkness bloomed a scene: all velvet and golden with dark obscure corners. "Rembrandt's *Holy Family*," said the announcer in his deepest voice. It seemed to reverberate beyond the amphitheater, out toward the coastal hills. Eva leaned toward my father.

"God forbid she's in some Christian picture," she said.

"Ssh," said my father. "I'll tell you when I see her."

On it went. Three ballerinas at the barre, each with a glowing face, a black band at the neck, a long salmon-pink leg in elevée, reflected in a mirror. A marble bas-relief of soldiers rushing into battle, the living figures looking precisely like stone. Eva gasped, and I saw that she was not yet swept up in the illusion, but was worrying that a player might lose his balance and tumble down onto the stage.

The Family of the Infante Don Luis was next: this was the one I had chosen for the deception, in case my father asked. Gold, pumpkin, dark green, an impromptu scene of family life at whose center sits a woman, having her hair done. On one side of her, the family maids bear aloft trays of gold-frilled lace and black-lacquered boxes. Between their skirts stands a little girl, her attention clearly caught by something off in a corner. On the other side, a group of courtiers in maroon frock-coats and green breeches look on with broad smiles or hostile, sneaky looks; surely they're plotting. The Infante Don Luis is an old prince, bewigged and worn down, seated at the same table where his wife, draped in white, is having her long hair dressed. She is absolutely the center, pale-lit against the tapestry of household chaos, her face deep in some private absorption made possible only by the activity around her. I liked this: the busyness all around, the stillness at the center.

Eva seemed to like it too; she relaxed again in her seat. She turned to my father and smiled. "That's her," she said. "I'd know her anywhere."

"I don't think so," said my father. "You forget, I know her too."

Several pictures later my father began to shift in his seat. "That's not her either," he said. "She's not that tall." His forehead looked waxy, ivory-blue in the twilight.

That was when the curtain went up on the last tableau.

"Cellini's *Golden Salt-cellar,*" said the announcer. A gasp came up from the audience as the golden crown slowly turned. There was Neptune, healthy and muscular, lazily leaning back, while Ceres held herself carefully erect. Just as in the picture my mother and I had been shown, Ceres looked less comfortable, and more alert than Neptune—you could see she was waiting for something. I could not, somehow, believe this was really my mother: she had never let me see her undressed, and yet, to my amazement, there were her breasts, and her slightly rounded belly, all so golden that I had to take it on faith that she was real. Did it really take so little to make the familiar world vanish—even those closest to you? I wanted to cry: there was something so sad and generous about her body: beauty, finally, was not exactly the thing. "Goddess of the Corn," said the announcer, "Ceres spent years searching for her daughter Persephone, who was abducted by the King of the Underworld. Cellini captured her grace and grief in this spectacular *Salt-cellar*—"

During the applause, I turned to see how my father was reacting to it. Like me, he'd been leaning forward, utterly absorbed. "Fantastic," he whispered. "You'd never recognize them in street clothes."

The curtain came down, and the crowd rose to its feet. He stood up, too, and stretched. I studied his face, but it gave nothing away. "So, kiddo," he said. "She's got me baffled. You can tell me now, which one was she in?"

"The Goya," I said quickly.

"Ah, *The Family of the Infante Don Luis*," he said, smiling down at me. "That would be one with the old prince looking wiped out, and the painter hiding behind the curtain."

"What painter?" I said.

"You didn't notice him," he said. "Funny, hardly anybody does."

"But you did," I said.

"So, I'm entitled. Certain things you start to notice, late in the game. It's a mystery to me, too, why it takes so long."

"I want to see those things too," I said. "I don't want to wait."

"You have to," he said. "That's the beauty of it." He was smiling, but his eyes were glassy bright. "Don't be in a rush, Rachel," he said. "When it's time, you'll know."

"Dad—" I started.

"No more questions for tonight," he said. "I'm out of steam."

As we left the Festival Grove that night, I noticed, on my mother's cheek, a crescent of gold paint. I imagined her at the dressing-room mirror, dabbing at her face with cold cream so no trace of her secret identity would be left. Had she been careless, hurried a little at the end, or was this a moment she couldn't resist, a private gift to my father? The two of them walked ahead of Eva and me, arm in arm, and though neither of them spoke, I felt they were at peace. And surely, if I'd been granted to see it, so had he: that faint glittering curve on her pale skin as we passed under ordinary streetlights. I took it as a sign that he knew the truth of who she'd been, and was content, for he hummed an old show tune as we walked back to the car. But just before he opened the door, he leaned toward her and said, "I've never seen you so beautiful. I'm right, aren't I? Were you who I think you were?"

She raised her face to his and smiled, and I marveled at how gracefully they moved past the question, neither of them giving away how much, or how little, they knew.

GRAVITY

At the last minute, he wanted his ashes flung out over the Pacific. "I've made the arrangements," he said, handing her a business card. He'd scrawled notes all over it, the way he once had on cocktail napkins and the pure empty corners of her own things-to-do lists if she left them too near the telephone. He tended to the diagonal, the dizzying, and this time, miniature, like some last terrible secret to keep from her, a something that looked like nothing. He took a little air from the respirator tube. "It's an outfit in Tijuana, much cheaper this way. Former trick pilots, spotless records. Only one stipulation—the widow has to go up."

"Go up?" she said. "In what sense, go up?"

"Don't worry. They're fully equipped. Safety belts, just like in a car."

"Abe, wait—" she began.

He drummed his fingers on the coverlet; he hated to be held up. "You'll be cured for life," he said. "Kill two birds, one stone."

And just like that, he was gone.

YOU COULDN'T CALL IT FEAR OF FLYING, nor did acrophobia cover it, though it had simplified life with Abe to call it that. The truth was that when he dragged her up to some lookout, she could only look down, and then she felt it: at first just a light wind against the backs of the knees, it crept upward like a seducer's hand between her thighs until she burned with the fierce secret ache of unsolved love, and not for him, exactly.

Maybe it was something that came with marriage. Nobody'd warned her; who'd have thought to? She was just a girl from Indiana, the flattest part—no bumps, no deviations, the eye went endlessly out, searching, not finding. He was her first city boyfriend, a blue-eyed Chicago boy with beautiful slender hands that shook for love. If she wouldn't neck with him, he'd lie down on her mother's couch and close his eyes, his arms folded tight across his chest—hours he could stay there, just to show her. He'd been raised in a sixth-floor walk-up, a narrow slot of brick out his childhood window, a flock of laundry headed south; the day she saw it, something knocked and shattered in her heart, and she raised her face to his, relenting. That was when he told her what he wanted from his life: to be rich, and to live on an ocean cliff, with the biggest windows money could buy. He loved surprises—didn't everyone?

For the honeymoon, he drove her straight to Niagara. That was where she got her first hint, there on the narrowest, oldest bridge he could find, so close to the Falls that the mist was no mist, but flung itself violently at them, sheet after sheet of fat needles. The men wore black slickers, the women, yellow—they huddled, turned back, they looked like bees ruined in the rain. At last, only she and Abe and the tour guide were left. "1883," he shouted to them over the roar. "Railing's fragile, just don't lean." Abe was trying to tell her something too, he waved his camera high. To hell with them both, she thought, and gave into it, fingers gripped to the splintery wood, knees yearning into the spaces between, so wide, so nothing. She looked down, and felt it again, felt herself open like a child's palm giving a surprise.

"Smile," he cried, and she nearly fell. It was no bridegroom's face she saw, but a huge mechanical eye in a dark hood.

"No more heights," she said.

"Stick with me," he said. "Maybe you'll get used to it."

It became, for him, a minor ambition to see her cured. Medical doctor, financial whiz, curer of wifely phobias. For their fifth anniversary he chose Rio, the Amazon route, and made her take the window seat: first view of the lightning, then the sudden quiet as they hung, then hurtled briefly toward the trees. She gripped the armrests, felt the sweet careening come her way, and closed her eyes for this unearthly love. "We'll be fine," he whispered. "What's one engine out of two?" For their tenth, he drove her along the California coast at its most curved, most precipitous—had he consulted with experts ahead of time? She could see him pacing in some cramped tourist office, his hands forever worrying the bright magazines, the neatly fanned brochures of possible bliss. "Where is it most dangerous, most steep," he'd cry. "I want my wife to see." What he wanted to show her, it turned out, was a particular cliff. There he took her arm and urged her toward its edge, toward the bronze plaque bolted into rock: *On this spot in 1892, a young bride tripped on her gown and plunged a thousand feet to the sea below.* According to legend the groom had tried to save her. No one blamed him, Abe said. Who could get a grip on all that satin?

It took a minute that time. She leaned, secret lover of vertigo, and almost let it take her. She saw herself, all that white tulle fluttering, falling, a bride in flight at last, like some fantastic crowned bird, the delicate slippers for once above, the veil below. It took her a minute to feel the change, like a shifting wind: Abe's hand no longer on her arm. Now she saw it, how he leaned away and pressed himself trembling to the rail as he once had to her hips, her waist, when they were young and she'd made him wait. She saw him as he'd been for maybe years, a figure in a doorway, his briefcase stuffed with papers like a prop, his blue eyes full of grief, and not for her, exactly.

"There's someone else," she said. "How long?"

"It was years ago," he said. "And no one since."

He leaned and leaned, he frowned at the rocks below in a way she feared and understood. How far can we go without going? Her heart fluttered cruelly, but she closed her eyes and pulled him back.

"Don't," she said. "Maybe you'll get over it."

They had their children, after all; he had his fortune, his house overlooking the sea. A view of big blue water, and as a concession to her, two heavy iron rails to keep the children from their deaths. It was all as he'd dreamed, like some terrible, purely American script nobody can ever alter. And it was there, one day, that her youngest—it is always the youngest—gazing dizzily down, gave it a try, slipping between the rails to swing herself out. "Mommy, Daddy, look at me." She hung out there where she shouldn't, where no grown person could wedge a shoulder through and pull her back. Surfers gathered below, holding beach towels taut, while Abe ran back and forth, thrusting his arms between the rails.

"I can't reach her," he cried at last. "Can you? I give you my word, my life, I'll change."

And so she knelt before the child, and felt it again: the old ache, but terrible this time, nothing sweet about it as it moved up from groin to belly, hollowing her out as she pried her daughter's fingers loose. Impossible, the strength of small fingers, the way a child looks at you, nodding yes but not letting go. She looks at you, knows you at last for the traitor you could be, even as you say it: "They'll catch you, sweetheart, I promise."

OVERHANGS, STADIUMS, a quaint Alpine tram swinging between Canadian cliffs during an unexpected storm. He caught her closing her eyes that time, saw the stiffness in her face as suffering, and wanted to send her to a specialist. He'd read in some book how they took you one step at a time. You approached your fear, fantasized it out; they gave you a little sedative if they had to. For heights, stairways were a nice start, he'd read. Also third-floor windows. *I'm fine*, she said, and hoarded it like a sweet mistake, a secret interlude all her own—a cool refusal he couldn't fight—

until she stood beside him once again, not on any cliff or lookout now, but in a little office whitely spare, with its four bright pictures of Pacific scenes, its neatly labeled drawers to chill the heart if you dared look down. The specialist was his, not hers; he clasped Abe's hands and held them longer than he should. "I won't make you sit for days and wonder," he said. "I'll tell you what we know."

The room she got him was high up, high as she could get, with a view toward the ocean, though the window bed was taken: there was nothing they could do. He looked at her, his eyes too bright, and she nearly saw it with him then: the story of his life. "It doesn't matter," he said. "I've seen what's to see."

She sat with him days, the pale blue curtains, like substitute skies, drawn all around. He strained to sit forward, weakly fell back.

"I know I let you down," he said. "Now I'm paying."

"Don't," she said, and pulled the curtain on its ratchety silver hoops, lifted him forward to look at what he could, a corner of a window out, a slice of blue. She held him until she felt at last, not the ruin but the grand and lonely ache of him that had been there all along, waiting for her in its sad blue depth. She bowed her head and prayed he'd never know: she'd never made it down that far.

BY THE DAY OF THE SERVICE, everybody knew his last desire. Family and friends surrounded her, came to hold her icy hands. They looked distracted, rushed through their grief to get her to the plane on time—he hated to be held up. She got last-minute advice, from the scientific to home remedies. Don't look up, don't look down, pinch the skin of your wrists three times each, count the numbers on the pilot's dash. Imagine the worst: abductions, engine failure, pilots with heart attacks. Imagine it all ahead of time, dare it to happen, and it never will. Some of the ladies told her not to go. "You're pale," they said. "You'll be sick. Let the pilot take him up alone—Abe'll never know." She shook her head; she wasn't so convinced.

At last, the service over, her daughter drove her to the airport where a man in sunglasses, all in blue, stood beside a plane. He held up a grocery sack, and bowed in a courtly way.

"Go," she said to her daughter. "I'm fine."

He was slim and olive-skinned, with a big mustache. He was as old as Abe. He'd been handsome once, was handsome still— there was no way around it.

"Señora, you have my sympathies," he said. He handed her the sack.

"That's him?" she asked.

"Sometimes in death, they seem bigger," he said. "I have taken the liberty to double-bag. Shall we go?"

TURBULENCE: SHE WAITS FOR IT, she has been told to imagine herself riding over the sea in a motorboat, riding a horse across a prairie. But there is no need: it is a dream of smooth rising, her body leans into the curve as if into a kiss. He talks to her through headphones, and there is nothing but the sudden sweet blur of his voice, a low hum beneath her thighs, the land curving away. A second steering wheel before her, but who needs that? She closes her eyes, a blue dream of forgetting, but no—in her lap is the sack, with its surprising heft and girth. They rise. The nose tips up until there is only sky, then down again, only by now, the water no longer looks like water. It's a blue cotton sheet that needs ironing, a scrap of holiday tinfoil left too long in the drawer. An island appears, a piece of old wedding cake detached and floating off. He is reaching over, putting her hands to her separate wheel. "Try it," he says. "Take us up." How long this lasts she can't say, only that she sees his own hands on his wheel again, feels the pull and veer against her own.

"Is it time?" she asks.

"Not yet," says the pilot. "Now for some serious climbing."

She sees Abe then, sees him clearly in an office, writing out his note, like a prescription in his doctor's scrawl. "Take her up," it says. "A little higher than she wants to go."

"Thanks, I've climbed enough," she says, and flips the window latch. Only she hasn't counted on the wind, the way it goes in a circle, reaches right into the plane for the sack. She lifts it barely, and it seems to open on its own, and there is something like snow, sharp like chipped paint against her eyes, swirling around her. In her ear the pilot murmurs, "Dios," and then the sky is the ocean, the ocean the sky, and the pilot's face close to hers and upside down, his sad gray mustache a beautiful upturned mouth. The stuff is on his dark glasses, on the dash, tapping against the windows, in her hair and thick against her mouth.

"Señora, hold on," he cries, and there is a moment, a stillness, then the whole coast comes out to meet her, a swooping arm of land across her face.

It lasts as long as a dream: is that what time is to the dead?

Because Abe is everywhere and nowhere now, a blue desire uprooted and dislodged. Whatever wish was trapped in him at birth has scattered as far as it will go.

"Steady, mi amor," says the pilot.

The sky above, the sea below. They are where they should be, but she shivers. She can't be sure she heard.

"You went too early," he cries.

"No," she says. "You waited too long."

And though there is nothing left in the bag, she shakes it out over the water, then lets the whole thing go, with a violence he cannot mistake.

A GHOSTLY GRIT OF ASHES will be on her mouth for days after—it's an illusion she cannot shake. In the quiet high house, the waves banging against the base of the cliff, she puts her finger to her lips to brush the feeling off, but it won't go. She lies down and Abe is there, a boy sitting forward on a couch, his mouth on her neck, her own nervous laugh, her hands pushing his shaking ones away. He is forever circling around her; she is forever putting him off, looking out over some other edge. Do the dead seek to be forgiven, or to forgive? What will send him on? She closes her eyes against the sight of his ocean, and remembers herself back inside the little plane, listening to the pilot's voice, the pilot's words, unreasonably tender against the muffled roar. The telephone is ringing; she is trying to rise—it might take years to get there. "Hello," she says, eventually. It will always be faint at first, that sound like drifting snow, that tells her it's coming from a long way off, before the voice itself tips toward her ear. "Are you there?" says the pilot, and she cannot help but answer. Of the two stages of descent, it is the sudden updraft of desire that always takes her by surprise. The pull of the earth never does.

MALINGERER

Pretend, produce, or protract, illness in order to escape duty (esp. of soldiers, sailors, etc.).
—*The Concise Oxford Dictionary*

*T*ake my advice: save your biggest secret till you're well beyond the grave.
The first reason is obvious: who can deny the dead forgiveness? In time,
a certain relenting enters the heart, though I can hear you saying, "Sure, you're
such a brave ghost, go visit Mom." I might—give me a minute. But the other
thing is this: the ache of the kept secret in life is not unlike the homesickness
after; the fullness of grief comes right back, very gorgeous and pure, minus
guilt, regret. These, it turns out, are decoration merely. Not that I don't have
my regrets, Daughter, don't get me wrong. I want to say first off I miss you all,
you and Gabe and your mother. But God help me, I miss the other lady too.

———

In the beginning, there was darkness—it should go without saying. Then light, yellow as lemons behind the eyelids, and a quiet like none he'd ever known. Lifelong dweller in cities, my father shivered: what else but death could produce such silence, such silky air? A bluejay screamed, then came a sound like summer camp: young male voices, a chorus of them, shouting. In one ear a tiny ocean swayed, muffled, soft. It took him forever to open his eyes, but even this was not so terrible. A new sensation, a luxury.

Two squares of blue: one chalky, one dark, in a white frame. Bars of blue shadow on hot white. His heart swelled to accept beauty as it always had, and in answer came a dark-haired child, a little girl. She wasn't his—he remembered now his Gabe, far away and waiting—but she flirted with him so boldly from under her big nurse's cap, she could have been.

"Hello, angel," he croaked, but her expression didn't change. She held, very soberly, an enameled bowl. A woman's voice called out, "Cecilia!" and as the child turned, light glinted off the bowl in one long slash. He had to close his eyes again. It felt dangerous to do so, a monumental act but without pain, but this time he understood. The word *pain*, traveling through him in its rickety carriage, made him know it was gone.

"So," he said. "Are you my Florence Nightingale?"

Her eyes opened wide. "Mami," she cried. Where was he, in what country? "Mami, I made the soldier come alive!"

"I'm not really a soldier. A doctor, actually—"

But she was gone, leaving light to break over him in golden flakes. A woman stood before him now, dark-haired like the child, her eyes the rich wet green of olives. She wore a nurse's white dress, but no nurse's cap. She carried no basin, no blood-pressure cuff. This would haunt him thereafter: that from the beginning, she had none of the stuff of modern medicine upon her.

"First time to California, Captain?" she asked, in the same accent as the child. She held up his chart, her pencil poised and tapping. "*Complete bed rest.* That's too bad, the weather's nice. But here I see *fresh air,* underlined twice. Somebody must like you."

Even holding still, a sense of flight. The wristbone so delicate he wanted to circle it, experimentally, with his fingers.

"Is this California?" he asked.

"You can look out the window, if you want." She reached forward to take his arm, to help him sit. "You should know the other men are jealous. They want to know how come you got the window seat."

Which was the dream: in here with her, or out on that grassy lawn? There, a group of men in khaki trousers, bare-chested, each with a cast on a leg or an arm—even around the ribs—raised their arms in a kind of Broadway unison, their leader invisible to him. There was general laughter, and then, from one young guy, a slight moan. "Sorry, sir," he said to the invisible leader, and my father's heart tightened. A shadow of the old pain crept forward, and withdrew.

"The boys from orthopedics," she said. But she was pointing beyond them all, to a red-tiled roof, a chalky blue sea.

"So that's the great Pacific," he said. "Where in California did you say—"

"I didn't," she replied. "I never do." From her skirt pocket she took a thermometer, shook it down, popped it in his mouth. "How can I cure you if you're talking?" she said, and took his wrist, all business.

He learned to expect her at the same time each morning, just as the blue bars of shadow struck the bright wall, and the men from the orthopedic ward went out for their morning calisthenics on the lawn. The ward door opened and the child Cecilia marched in first, the mascot before the parade. There was, each time, a ritual scattering of applause from the beds, and she took a little bow, then held the door open for her mother, who appeared sometimes in white, other times with a Red Cross apron over her skirt and blouse. But never a cap, never the Army Nurse Corps insignia. His nearest neighbor, a pale Nevada kid named Roy Parvis, had told him what he knew: she was a civilian nurse's aide, Red Cross trained. Not official Army, but the real thing, best nurse in the whole joint. "She's one of those healer-people," said the kid. "I saw one at work in Luzon—they have 'em, you know, down there. Only ours, she's different. Cures you by breaking the heart. You fall in love, and bam, your circulation improves. The only problem comes later."

"Why?" said my father. "What happens then?"

"Nothing," said Parvis, with a sigh. "Goddamned nothing."

The ritual went like so: the child moved from bed to bed, offering a single pink candy pill to each man. Anyone who could, lifted an arm to receive her pretend blood-pressure cuff. My father waited in his Gatch bed by the far window—this was the price for the window seat, he understood, to wait patiently while the angels ministered elsewhere. While he waited, Parvis sniffed at the sea air as if taking what was left. "Luzon, my God. Hell itself. Where were you, Captain Gershon?"

"Zone of Interior, Hospital Train #1," my father replied, blushing. "I don't know how I rate the window."

"I'm sure you did something," said Parvis. "You're a doc, I heard. We appreciate you guys, all of you." He raised his hand, barely, to signal that he had to stop. It didn't matter: they both knew they were really waiting for her, watching her slip between the beds after Cecilia, offering a murmur each man craned to hear. She gave presents, too, though these were small things, he was glad to see: a set of comics, a book from the hospital library. Depending on the day, some men got a shampoo and shave, with Cecilia's enameled bowl and a jug of water. It was like no hospital, like no army he'd ever known. Any minute he'd have to wake up, and it would all disappear.

But not yet. The light held, and so did her voice, and that was how my father came to learn the story of his own illness as if it were a fairy tale, told by a mother to her little girl. "Listen, Cecilia, once upon a time a doctor got sick tending soldiers on a train. But there was evil on this train, because sometimes in real life bad men come, *mi hija*, not just in stories," and when she said this, he remembered the morning he couldn't get up, how another medical officer shook him, or was it the train itself? He couldn't tell. *I'll flatten you like an ant, you Jewish fake*, said a voice he didn't know. *Get up and get moving.* A hallucination, surely.

But this much was in the train log they received, she said, a single line: *Captain Abe Gershon, Hospital Train #1, Zone of Interior, Malingerer.* The initials below illegible. Next thing, another medic found him passed out in his bunk, his fever at 104, the left ear badly infected, who knew how long?

"He's the one who saved you," she told him now, very softly, her hand on his. "Without him, you know, more than the hearing in that ear would be gone. A good man, he should get a medal, only he didn't give his name. Just got you to us, fast as he could."

"What's yours," he asked. "Name, I mean."

"Carmen," she replied, laughing. "But don't worry. I'm nothing like the famous one."

YOU SEE HOW THINGS START, RACHEL, *in beauty, innocence? She was right about the records: years later I dug around, and found the note in the Medical Department Archives. Just my name and rank, the word* Malingerer, *and the illegible initials. Maybe she was right: whatever evil blows through the world touched that train, and moved on. Evil, or maybe fate, I can't help thinking. Because this was the turn in my life, after which everything changed, and why I could never explain to your mother...honest to God I didn't arrange it! To nearly die, to be nursed back to health by a woman named Carmen, the one who healed, it was said, by breaking the heart for good. I tried to find her later too, I confess. Years after, but listen, in the archives there's no record of her, or of the child, either. Apparently they didn't keep records of the volunteers, the civilian aides—there were thousands, they said, it would have been a bureaucratic nightmare. This nice librarian, oh, she looked at me politely enough, but I knew she thought I was cracked. "Of course you know it has never been the Medical Department's policy to allow a child the run of our facilities, even in one of our wartime convalescent*

194

centers, Doctor, relaxed as they were. Did you say the woman was of Hispanic descent? Doubtless, then, she was a civilian, a local housemaid perhaps, whose domestic skills were welcome in those times. Severe shortages in the Army Nurse Corps, if you understand me....:"

Listen, Rachel. Let's say you could cross one of those sleazy wartime fantasies with a sad true story by Chekhov. That's the one I'm trying to tell: equal parts dream and disappointment, and somewhere in the mix a mystery, a thing absolutely real, and forever lost. I lay the fantasy part to my upbringing: my mother told me tales of my childhood like she was reading from a famous guy's biography, so I grew up believing my life had a shape, very dramatic. For example, once upon a time, when I was but six months old, I was kidnapped! Stolen by shady Mafioso characters from a railway carriage for ransom, in the one moment she took a breath of her own and hustled to the john. Fantastic—apparently they mistook me for a celebrated infant. How was I rescued? By the miracle of disgust, of course: left in another railway carriage, a big you-know-what in my diapers. God, she loved to tell this one—at card parties, at public parades! It seems the kidnappers realized their mistake around the time I crapped my pants, or maybe it's just that for this eventuality they weren't prepared. Your mother never appreciated this one—it was too low-class for her. So maybe also I'm telling you this by way of showing our difference. Maybe it'll help you sort it out. Maybe not.

On the third morning Carmen handed him a postcard. "Write something nice to your wife." He turned it over. On the front, an Indian maiden with long dark braids stood before an old mission church, a basket of oranges on her arm.

Out of his mouth, the first surprise. "You know," he said. "You resemble this girl."

She frowned, tapped her foot. "The Ward Nurse has sent

your wife word that you are out of danger, and will be home after a period of recovery, two weeks, maybe three. Now, Captain, write something nice."

"Call me Abe," he said. "And I'm sorry, I didn't mean—"

But she was still tapping her foot, waiting. Was he really too weak to hold the pen? She agreed to take dictation, which kept her there a little longer. Though the whole time, he noticed, she looked away, never out the window, but always down the ward with its row of beds, each with its exercise pulley, or a puzzle spread out on the blanket; the constant low hum of voices, rustlings. Always some movement or other caught her eye, and up went her head, alert as a cat's. He knew he shouldn't, but he liked what happened when she was detained: the subtle flickering of her jaw muscle, her fingers lightly trembling. She couldn't wait to get away, and yet—. He looked out the window, but it was too late: his skin was warm, every nerve alive.

"Okay, I'm ready," he said. "My dear Clara. Weak as an old fish, left ear in trouble, but glad to be alive. You should see this place. Like a spa, with guys out on the lawn doing push-ups—only in a cast. They say you can take flute lessons, or a foreign language—should I? Anyway, there's too much light; makes me miss Indiana. Love and hot tamales, your lonesome swain, Abe."

"Hot tamales?" she said. "Lonesome swain?"

He smiled at her. "Should I tone it down?"

She stood abruptly, shrugged. "You know best," she said, and was gone.

"Nurse Carmen, come back," he cried. But she'd vanished, leaving only silence and her anger, like a scent he couldn't be sure of, but ached to smell again. Parvis was awake, fanning himself in mock distress. "Open the window wider, Doc, before you burn us both up."

My father heard this, but only faintly—Parvis, and the rest of the ward, was on his left, his bad ear side, and it was easy to pretend he hadn't, to let himself drift in the sweet ache of her walking away like that, until the ward doors opened again, and the rumbling of the food carts began. That was another ritual: the chorusing of men, all sitting up or standing beside their beds, all wanting to know what's on the menu today. Then he noticed Roy was gone, the bedsheets crumpled and empty. Heart thrumming, he called out to the guy in the next bed over.

"Where'd Parvis go?" he cried. "Is he okay?"

The soldier laughed. "You bet he is," he said. "Our Roy's been gone an hour—to Spanish class with Señora Carmen. Can you beat this country?"

"Private, or group?" said my father, heat flaring in his wrists and arms. He remembered what Parvis had said, and sat up a little straighter. "No, you sure can't," he said humbly. "Speaking of our great nation, can you tell me where we are, exactly?"

The soldier smiled. "San Luis Obispo, they call it," he said. "But don't tell her I told you."

DAUGHTER, I HAVE NEVER THOUGHT OF MYSELF *as a man talented in the arts of love. When I was fifteen, Mama sent me to the neighborhood prostitute, who owed her a favor. She had other, paying customers waiting, but figured it wouldn't take long. I was not to linger, my mother said, sending me off, she's a busy woman and I don't want her to feel I've taken advantage.*

What do I remember? Squalor, chiefly: a stained tablecloth, a half a cup of tea left out. By the bed, a bottle of medicine, a dirty spoon. For anything the place was like a lousy downtown clinic, no funding, and she the lone beleaguered nurse. "We don't have all day," she said, sighing. "How's your Mama's gout?" At any rate, she didn't require much of me… did this make me an impatient husband? Maybe if I'd gone to a ritzier outfit?

And what about your beautiful mother, schooled the opposite way? On our wedding night her mother gave her this advice: "It hurts less if you hold still." So she did. And there she was, a lovely red-haired girl, her skin the palest gift I'd ever seen.

Daughter, I was ever a gambler, and you may find, someday, you have a streak of this yourself. When I courted your mother, I had the sense I was risking all in a great gambit. She was above me in class and culture, and smarter in everything—okay, except maybe finance. To win her was to win some war I'd been fighting all my life. You know her bearing, her style. She had to come down a couple levels to meet me; okay, sure, a medical student with a good future ahead, but from a lousy family, if you know what I mean. It was a gap we were proud of, in our young way. Me, especially. I thought I'd created my life, but the truth is, all design is fraud, cover-up, a monstrous mistake we make again and again until we die.

TOO MUCH LIGHT. Had he really written that? Still, it wasn't untrue. There were times he missed, sharp and sudden as a taste, the dark of winter dusk in Indiana, Clara's bright head bent over the piano in their rented house.

But in the mornings, now, he was starved only for light, craved it like food: the way it rested on windowsills and the child's black hair, on Carmen's clipboard and wristwatch, her swift fingers. It was his second week, and he was "allowed to perambulate, within reasonable limits." He took his daily constitutional, as Carmen called it, up and down the ward.

"Captain," a man would shout from his bed. "How are the seas today?"

"Light breeze, good sailing," he'd shout back, and they'd both salute. Amazing, there was no ill will—nobody really begrudged him his window—but this, too, seemed temporary, something that would have to end with the war.

One day the child didn't come, and when Carmen appeared at his bedside, he asked her shyly if she could wheel him out on the lawn. "Remember my chart?" he said. "I'm supposed to have lots of fresh air."

Did he imagine her hesitation? Never mind. He sat up boldly in his bed, to show her he was ready. "Bring on the dragon lady. Let her judge for herself."

"It's not that," she said. "But maybe somebody else should take you out."

"I don't want to go if it's not you," he said, with Gabe's pout.

She sighed; she was a mother, after all. "I'll find out," she said. "Don't be in such a hurry."

Of course, his wish was granted, and he had to brush aside the uncanny feeling that they were afraid to deny him, that while he was there—and only there—he could have anything he wanted. Out they went, and halfway across the grassy lawn, he had the terrible urge to see how tall she was, or rather, to see how her height matched his. He said, as neutrally as he could, that maybe he could try walking a few steps, she didn't need to baby him. But she shook her head. He would have to get the Ward Nurse's permission for that, she said. Besides, the staff didn't want patients strolling the grounds in pajamas and robe.

"I'll get permission, then. One more question. When are you at liberty?"

She sighed again, but didn't resist. "I get off work at seven, if that's what you mean."

He bowed his head. "I would be honored if you would walk with me. My intentions are honorable."

She laughed. "You're a married man; they better be. Are you feeling all right? Any delirium?"

"I don't know," he said. "In my other life, I'm not this way."

"How are you, in your other life?" She was suddenly serious.

"I wish I knew," he said. "Not like this."

HE KNEW BETTER THAN TO BOTHER with the Ward Nurse. He went straight to the Chief Medical Officer, and introduced himself as the fellow from Hospital Train #1, the ear case. The Colonel, a doctor himself, rose to shake his hand, and said a little too heartily, "I'm glad to meet you, Captain Gershon. I've wanted to say, for some time now, we are all so sorry about the ear. The Medical Department is making every effort to track down the fellow who misdiagnosed—" The Colonel tapped his pencil, lifted papers and put them down.

"What's done is done," replied my father, making his voice as humble and modest as he could. He was beginning to see how he'd gotten the window, the fancy Gatch bed, everything. "Colonel, Sir,

I appreciate the fine treatment I have received here, and hope it won't be too much to ask one more favor—"

"Ask away," said the Colonel. "Given the circumstances, we can bend the rules a little."

So it came to be written in his chart, that he could "perambu-late," out of doors each day at dusk, twenty minutes, under the supervision of a nurse's aide or Red Cross volunteer. On the first day, he must start in the wheelchair, and sit back down at the slightest hint of weakness. Civilian clothes permitted. He was not, after all, a prisoner, said the Colonel. Dismissing my father, he winked as if they'd cut a deal of some kind, or as if, in fact, my father was a prisoner, a slightly dangerous one.

"Enjoy your evening walks, Captain," said the Colonel. "But don't crow about them to the others, if you know what I mean."

AT THE APPOINTED HOUR, Carmen met him at the ward entrance with a wheelchair. It was dusk, and chilly; she wore a pale blue sweater over her dress. "I don't have long," she said, and he nodded, chastened as a child who knows now, absolutely, that he has received more than his share. But he was aware, too, of a hunger for sensation that felt new, and right. Sounds, particu-larly, made him ache to know more: were they distant or close? As she wheeled him out onto the sidewalk, he thought he heard the crash of surf, and farther off, a band tuning up, the cry of a child floating up like a kite string. There were new smells, too: the saltiness in the air, a flowering bush that smelled like an orange. "Where's the beautiful Cecilia tonight?" he asked.

"My mother's watching her," Carmen said, and her voice in his good ear was kind, the stiffness and anger gone.

"I hear a band," he said. "Is there a concert?"

She frowned. "You can be out twenty minutes. That's all."

She insisted he stay in the wheelchair until they get to the park.

"I confess I found out where we are," he said.

"Ah," she said. "Cheating."

"San Luis Obispo," he cried. "Am I in trouble now?"

"Yes," she said sternly. She had come around in front, to straighten the blanket on his lap, he guessed, to tuck him in more securely. Impulsively, he made a little wish: *Look at me. I won't ask anything else, I promise.* But when she did, her gaze, so direct and unexpected, rushed straight down into him and took everything away.

"Hold out your hands," she said. "And I'll help you up."

Wait, he wanted to whisper, can we go back to the minute just before? Because he knew what was coming now. That was the cruelty of the granted wish. As she helped him up, his skin tightened, and heat brushed through him like fire, leaving nothing but a pile of ash in place of his heart.

If she noticed, she gave no sign, only led him across the grass toward a gazebo, where five men, all in Navy blues and sunglasses, were tuning up, playing little riffs. On the grass was a scattering of soldiers, and more arriving, on crutches, or wheeled out in chairs. Those who could walk looked slightly embarrassed, their shoulders curving in, as if they hoped to make themselves look smaller, less fit. Three naval nurses, all in dark blue, had spread a blanket, laughing.

Suddenly the band veered into life: two trumpets and a saxophone, a clarinet and drums, all on a careening ride to nowhere. There was something strange about them, something he couldn't quite figure out.

"Carmen," he said. "Is there something wrong with this band?"

"Not wrong," she said. "But definitely different." At last she smiled. "C'mon, can't you see it?" she said. "Keep looking."

It was watching the drummer, finally, that made him see it. Something about the way he held his elbows so tight to his ribs, like he'd moved all the pieces in nice and close. "Am I right," he said. "Are they all blind?"

"Fantastic," she said, breaking into applause with the rest. "Every single one of them."

"Carmen," he whispered. "How come nothing seems real out here?" And then, he couldn't help it, he put his hand on her wrist. "Are you?"

"I am," she said, in a ragged, joyful voice. "I wish I weren't."

THE NEXT MORNING, he dictated another postcard. "Carmen, take this down," he said, as if he were at his office at home. "Darling," —a little shock rolled through him at the new sound of the word in his mouth—"Darling, the strangest thing of all: a blind band has formed among the recuperating men. Last night they played your favorites—Irving Berlin, George Gershwin. No Mozart for these guys, though. It's all jazz."

He told himself he wanted to please Clara, make sure she knew he was thinking of her, but the truth hung before him, strict and unrelenting. He was a spoiled child, an infant trying to manipulate the clouds. The world would have to deny him, and soon. But she—Carmen—wasn't walking away, not yet. Finishing the note, she looked at him fully, tenderly, as if she had seen for herself his weakness, its hidden cave, and was not appalled. For the first time, he saw it too, and felt not so much forgiven as accepted; she had seen his weakness as grief, the wavering core of him as a thing to be nursed and loved. But if this was what it meant to be healed, why did desire awaken, too? Who was strong enough to pull the two apart; take the knowledge, and not the longing to spring free of the old life? Who was strong enough to go home cured, when home itself seemed to have vanished?

Exquisite inadvertence. They did not agree to meet at the gazebo, but at the beginning of his third week, dressed and walking on his own, he found her there. Cecilia was with her, and when she saw him, she gave a little cry and ran from her mother to him. He couldn't help himself: he squatted down and opened his arms. The warmth, the hunger of the child made sense to him now, and he remembered Gabe, the way he cuddled, loverlike, in Clara's arms. Here, at last, were the possibilities of his own body: its capacity for warmth, for the giving and receiving of tenderness, and he was astonished, grateful for the tiniest chance to use it. Why hadn't he known it before—how dangerous, and how necessary it was to put your face in a child's hair, warmed from the sun, and gaze up at her mother? Her mother, whose face showed everything plainly now: a burning pleasure, a rising fear.

"Cecilia," she said. "Please leave the doctor alone." And she looked at him, her eyes bright with tears.

BACK IN THE WARD THAT NIGHT, he was barely in bed when Roy Parvis leaned his way.

"Hey, Doc," he said, his voice hushed and amazed. "There's a bet down the line. First the window, now Carmen. Is it true the Colonel gave you some special deal? How much *dinero?*"

"What do you mean—she's our nurse!" my father cried. Anger swirled in him, a sickly green. But Roy Parvis was red with shame. He had said it all in the kindest tone, with a kind of awe. "They asked. I told 'em I'd try to find out. No hard feelings, Doc?"

"I guess not," said my father. "But goddamn it, tell them it's not true. Would you, Parvis? I'd be grateful."

"Nada," he said. "They're just jealous."

Did you know, Rachel, that I was on leave, just for a weekend before I got on that train, and wound up here? My last night, I begged of your mother a little favor—this you could guess, if you do the math. Our last night in the cottage all to ourselves, before she went to stay at your Grandma Eva's, and I headed out again. I wanted her—I always wanted her, never think otherwise. And did she want me? Of this, I'm less sure. I can't say, I never could, with her. But she let me approach, and in the midst of it all, I remember, she looked at me the strangest way, through me, I think, and out the other side, as if she saw her life beyond me, without me. I shivered, it was another kind of knowledge, like an edge so sharp and bright I had to shut my eyes. We didn't know it, of course. But in that gaze, Daughter, you were conceived. All the time I was gone, in that other world, you were coming to life. Oh, I wish I'd known.

———

He tried to convince himself that it meant nothing. They couldn't help what they felt, but they could keep it innocent, right? If we just sat on the grass, if we just met here by accident. She had her blanket, he had his. Cecilia ran wild in front of the gazebo, doing ballet for the officers, the nurses, then circled back to them and draped her whole body across their two laps, and tried to pull their heads together. "Kiss! Kiss!" she whispered. He looked around in terror, and so did Carmen, but no one seemed to care; they were all watching the band. Something ran through him then, impossible to describe. He was pure as beach sand, heated through, broken down to his molecules and reshaped. No one has seen, he said to himself. She herself had no idea of what had just gone through him. Nothing had happened, nothing would. It was possible to feel this way, and do nothing.

Except that at that very moment one of the trumpet players smiled directly at them, as if he were not blind at all, and pulled the band into "As Time Goes By." He and Carmen did not look at each other, but waited politely until the song was done, and folded their blankets without speaking. Neither of them spoke on the way back, but Cecilia wouldn't stop chattering. On the way back to the hospital grounds she reached up and took each of their hands in hers. "Swing me," she cried, and they did, back and forth, her sweet dark hair rising and falling against the blue.

"I will die because of you," said Carmen.

"I'll die first," he said.

"You both will," said the child, still swinging. "And I won't!"

"My God," she said.

"It's okay. Kids say all kinds of things."

"Not this kid. Not my Cecilia."

He looked around, but no one was there to hear. It was nearly dark, and the grassy lawn was unfathomably deserted. Then he heard, through his good ear, the clink of plates and silver—it was suppertime, they were all inside, that was all, it was nothing supernatural. He waited until the child was running again, out on the lawn, and then, in the space of one heartbeat, he pulled Carmen into his arms and back out again, away.

"I won't. Ever again," he said, and nearly ran from her. Stumbling back into the ward, walking down the long room past every man's bed, every man's eyes cast down to his plate, he knew, suddenly, what Cecilia meant. Never had anything been more certain, more true. He would get better because of her, and then later, when nobody was looking, he would die. Not obviously, not right away. But he knew now how it worked. How long it would take, he understood, was none of his goddamned business.

HE HAD THOUGHT IT SUMMER, by the air, but it was only April. April 24th, she told him, my day off, and tomorrow you will be discharged, and on your way home. She seemed oddly jubilant, and at the same time, very pale. But she told him how to sign out: to write a note requesting a one-day leave, to go into town to buy gifts for his family. "Meet me by the gazebo," she said. "I want to take you somewhere."

"Is Cecilia coming?" he asked shyly, knowing he shouldn't.

She shook her head. "This time, no Cecilia."

And so he did as she bade, and found her not far from the gazebo, leaning against a clean but aged green car, the engine humming.

"Where are we going?"

"You still haven't learned," she said.

"San Luis Obispo," he said proudly.

"Genius," she replied. "But that's not where we're going."

"I submit," he said, and bowed his head to hide his happiness.

Of course there were street signs, but as if in collusion with her, none of them helped; all were in Spanish; all were beautiful, and without meaning for him. He struggled to commit them to memory; they fled past him like a foreign prayer.

"Do you at least have a map I could look at?" he asked, after a while.

"I always get more lost when I use them."

The car wound upward through canyons, high into chaparral-laced hills and dry air. Cicadas buzzed, too, but only in the right ear.

"What, you are taking me to the place of execution?" he said.

She only smiled. He could not shock her; she seemed to know, ahead of time, what he would say. "You talk too much," she said lightly, and again he bowed his head. Not hurt, not even surprised. In her mouth the truth was comedy; he was refreshed.

At last they reached a summit, a hill among hills. How different the air was up there, and where, after all, were they? He looked about him for landmarks, imagined trying to find his way back to this spot in years to come, from the relation of the hills to the sea. But it was hard to concentrate, with the sunlight and the good breeze—the air itself took all of his attention, just to recognize how different it was from anything in his life so far. He wanted to tell Carmen this. To say how sharp and tangy the wind in the pines, how it made him glad to be with her.

"Look how far away everything is," she said. "Can you still hear the ocean?"

His heart pumped fast. "No," he said. "Is it just me, because of the ear?"

"No," she said. "No human can hear it from this far away."

"Can you?" he asked.

Later, he could not remember how she answered.

And did he himself speak again, that day? This memory, too, would vanish, cleanly erased. Did he actually ask, out loud, Carmen, will you lie down with me? And did she use words to answer him?

IN YEARS AFTER, he would not remember how it happened, only that it did, and that this much—whatever else was lost or unreal—remained true: her mouth and her fingers met his, and for a time, a delicate, dangerous surprise lived between them. Nothing could disturb his belief that she existed, and loved him on that hill, not even what happened the next day, when he found himself in the Colonel's office, signing the papers for his release.

He'd been worrying about her all morning. She hadn't come to the ward that day at her accustomed time, and nobody but him seemed the least dismayed. He had a little gift for Cecilia; a beaded bracelet he'd bought at the commissary. Now, in the Colonel's office, he saluted and said, "Sir, before I go, a last favor?

I need to give this to a nurse's aide from our ward, the girl named Carmen." He stopped suddenly. In all this time, he realized, he had neglected to ask her last name.

The Colonel was seated at his desk, surrounded by paper, and didn't seem to have heard him. Paper after paper had to be signed—a dream of paper, endless and unreal. That's how it happened that my father had time to look around the room; time to notice a poster on the wall, its corners curling inward from the damp ocean air. It was an advertisement for War Bonds: in it, a pretty young nurse leaned toward a man stretched out on a cot, a bandage around his head. The soldier gazed up at his nurse, and was consoled. No, it was more than that; he was falling in love. Because of her tenderness, he would live. It was a sentimental love story, embarrassing at any distance. But the whole nation hungered for it, thrived on it. And it wasn't exactly a lie, my father thought. What was true about it could not be spoken, that was all.

"Carmen wasn't in this morning," my father tried again, speaking her name as casually as he could manage. "Can you help me find her? I have a present for her little girl."

At last the Colonel glanced up from his endless paperwork. He smiled, got to his feet.

"Two things, Captain Gershon," he said. "First, I am glad you made such a fine recovery, that our convalescent center has been such a success in your case. Second, and don't get me wrong, Doctor, with a fever like yours, hallucinations aren't uncommon. A small price to pay for recovery. Damned near miraculous."

Then he saluted my father. "Welcome back to the world,

Captain. Safe journey home. And my father, saluting him back, had no choice but to go.

THE AUTHOR

Jeffrey Sklansky

Marjorie Sandor

is the author of *The Night Gardener,* essays (The Lyons Press, 1999) and *A Night of Music: Stories* (Ecco Press, 1989). Her short fiction has been anthologized in *Best American Short Stories* (1985 and 1988), *The Pushcart Prize XIII,* and *The Best of Beacon 1999,* and has appeared in such journals as *The Georgia Review, The Southern Review, The New York Times Magazine,* and elsewhere. Awards include a 1998 Rona Jaffe Foundation Award for Fiction, and the 2000 Oregon Book Award for literary nonfiction. She teaches creative writing and literature at Oregon State University in Corvallis, Oregon.